Bama Bob shook his lionlike head and declared, "If there is one thing I hates it's a mugwump who sits on the fence with his mug on one side and his wump on the other. But we might just let you live in exchange for some display of proper attitude. Why don't you just get down on one knee and offer us a sincere rendition of 'Dixie'?"

"From the heart, with feeling." His coyotegrinning pal tossed in for the amusement of the obviously rebel crowd assembled.

I unbuttoned my sheepskin jacket to clear the grips of my Walker Colt as I quietly said I wasn't much of a singer.

Bama Bob took a casual step clear of the bar as he stared at my gun instead of my face, saying, "Well, well, will you look at the big popgun they let this child out to play with."

Other gents began to crawfish back from the bar as the one in the bigger hat said, "If I was you, Tennessee, I'd do just like Bama Bob says. For anyone can see it's two against one here."

*Also by Lou Cameron:*

**THE HOT CAR**
**THE SPIRIT HORSES**
**STRINGER**
**STRINGER ON ASSASSIN'S TRAIL**
**STRINGER ON DEAD MAN'S RANGE**
**THE GRASS OF GOODNIGHT***
**THE BUNTLINE SPECIAL***
**CROOKED LANCE***
**YELLOW IRON***

*\*Published by Fawcett Books*

# EAGLE CHIEF

## Lou Cameron

FAWCETT GOLD MEDAL • NEW YORK

Now that we've saved the Union and no Indians have lifted hair in recent memory, a heap of folk who never rode with us sound mighty certain about the part the Colorado Volunteers played in that war we had between the states.

I wish I felt half so certain about next month's sales at the saddle shop I own on Larimer Street. But you see, I was there when Colonel John Chivington, the Preaching Militant of Denver, drew his terrible swift sword to smite the sins of the slavocrat and the savagery of the South Cheyenne and, to tell the pure truth, I'm still a mite confused. So I'll just tell the tale the way it happened and let you make up your own mind.

The war was a year old and I was pushing nineteen the night I first rode into Denver. I'd ridden all day and then some to make it just after sundown, with the Front Range looming inky-black against a bloodred western sky to my right. Most of the private housing and half the business structures were still canvas stretched over balloon framing. The lamps lit inside made them glow like big, square, paper lanterns. It was just as well, for as yet there wasn't a street lamp standing in the rough-and-ready little town.

I reined across from Wallington & Murphy's big frame store on 16th Street. That shows you how new I was in town. It looked like a smart enough place to stop, as green as I still was,

1

because a livery and saloon stood cheek-by-jowl on my side of the wide, dirt-paved thoroughfare. The livery offered fodder, water, and a safe stall for my tired mount. A sign out front of the saloon offered me a swamping stein of draft beer, brewed in the German fashion, for a reasonable-sounding two cents.

First things first, I made certain the pal I'd ridden all the way from the Mormon Delta was rubbed down, watered, and oated before I strode next door to wet my own whistle and, if they served it, put away some supper.

As I eased through the thin crowd and thick tobacco smoke toward the packing-case bar, I suspected I'd picked the wrong saloon. It stood smack in the center of town, yet I was getting those fish-eyed stares a stranger is more prone to attract in out-of-the-way dives frequented by moonshiners and road agents.

I'd have felt just as awkward had I simply spun around and run for it, thirsty. So I bellied up to the bar as bold as I could manage at that age and allowed I'd have one of them swell two-cent beers they had on tap.

There was a gilt-framed mirror on the wall behind the bar. So I got to admire my own poker face as the barkeep served me a mighty modest tumbler of beer, compared to what I'd seen on that sign out front.

The joke was on me, and nobody admires a poor sport. As I sipped what there was, I noticed they'd either let the mirror get mighty grimy or I needed a shave and a good going over with naphtha soap and a bristle brush after all those dusty days on the trail.

I was sort of proud I needed to shave most every other day, now, and I'd filled out a mite after my last growth spurt so's I didn't look quite as tall and skinny. We've never really decided whether the high cheekbones and sort of slanty gray eyes in the family come down to us from some remote redskin or the elfin Shee Folk who dwelt in the hills and hollows of the old country before more regular-looking humans showed up.

As skimpy as my beer was, I'd barely put away half of it when I was joined by two somewhat older and burlier gents. The one looming close enough for me to smell the rye whiskey on his breath was trying to look like an African lion, going by the way he'd let his dishwater-blond hair and whiskers grow. The even meaner-looking one on his far side reminded me of a coyote wearing a big Texas sombrero.

The one blowing whiskey fumes in my face announced, "I'd be Bama Bob Brodie from Montgomery Town and it's my considered opinion they ought to arrest Mary Todd Lincoln on a charge of public bestiality. For who can deny she's borne half-human sons to the one and original Honest Ape?"

I smiled back twice as sweet and replied, "I'd be Ross Clark from Cumberland County, Tennessee. We didn't live close enough to any town to matter. I came west back in Sixty to ride the mail for Russell, Majors, and Waddell."

The one in the bigger hat chimed in, "He means the Pony Express, Bama. Everyone knows who the damnyankee Pony Express rides for!"

I tried, "Not no more. Not since that Western Union outfit strung the last of their wondrous wires between Sacramento and Saint Joe. For there is just no way a pony can beat a dot or even a dash across all those dusty miles. So the company just filed for bankruptcy."

I finished the last of my bitty beer, put the empty glass down, and added in a desperately casual tone, "I was one of the first they laid off, as overweight, while they were still making money. So I was lucky. I fear some of the skinnier kids are never going to see their back wages."

Bama Bob looked me over from dusty boot tips to pancaked hat as he decided, "You don't look so weighty to me. I bet I got forty pounds on you. Where *do* you tip the scales, at say a hundred and fifty?"

I said, "That sounds close enough. Ain't been on any scales since they let me go such a long way from home with winter coming on. I know just a few pounds can make a big difference when you're charging by the ounce to deliver skinny letters but—"

"Let's talk politics," Bama Bob cut in, adding, "it's our understanding Tennessee rates a star on the new Confederate battle flag. On the other hand that scalawagging Governor

Johnson you Tennessee folk went and elected has come out in favor of the Union, the son of a bitch!''

His coyote-faced companion demanded, ''Is that any way for decent white folk to act? Everyone knows the mountain whites of Tennessee came up outten Georgia to take them hills from the Cherokee just one generation back!''

I didn't let on my own clan had moved into Cumberland County after Gramp Clark lost his original land in Kentucky, nor did I feel it wise to opine none of my kith and kin would have much use for an indentured darky if they'd been able to afford one. I said, ''Abe Lincoln went and appointed us a military governor. So no kin of mine ever voted for Andrew Johnson. I can't rightly say how many of my clan will end up on one side or the other. Tennessee boys are inclined to fight for or against anyone they've a mind to and, as for me, I haven't decided. That's one reason I haven't been anxious to head back home, yet. I'd surely hate to put a rifle ball in anyone without a better reason than I've heard the stump speakers for either side offer, up to now.''

Bama Bob seemed to consider my words and, for a moment, I thought I might have phrased things right. Then he shook his lionlike head and declared, ''If there is one thing I hates worse than a damnyankee it's a mugwump who sits on the fence with his mug on one side and his wump on the other. But we might just let you live in exchange for some display of the proper attitude. Why don't you just get down on one knee and offer us a sincere rendition of 'Dixie'?''

''From the heart, with feeling,'' his coyote-grinning pal tossed in for the general amusement of the obviously rebel crowd assembled.

I unbuttoned my sheepskin jacket to clear the grips of my cross-draw Walker Colt as I quietly said I wasn't much of a singer.

Bama Bob took a casual step clear of the bar as he stared thoughtfully at my gun hand instead of my face, saying, ''Well, well, will you look at the big popgun they let this child out to play with.''

Other gents began to crawfish back from not only the bar,

but the lamp-lit center of the saloon entire. The one in the bigger hat said, "You don't want to play that way with Bama Bob, Tennessee. If I was you I'd just do like he says. For anyone can see it's two to one here."

Then I flinched and almost let it show, when another voice rang out from behind me, "You're wrong, Steinmuller. I'm making it two against two and I'm betting them odds are too rich for you brave bummers."

Bama Bob scowled past me to demand, "What call have you to mix in this, Beckwourth? Might this Tennessee nigger-lover be kin to you?"

My as yet unseen comrade-in-arms chuckled dryly and said, "It's possible, on my daddy's side. Be that as it may, I'm going to count to ten, now. Do I have to tell you what I mean to do if either of you polecats are still within pistol range when I get done?"

He didn't. He'd barely counted to six before the two bullies who'd been rawhiding me were out of sight. Some of the others had left as well, shooting dirty looks our way as they'd departed the premises. The stranger who'd just saved my bacon said, "Them bummers might be back with others, and this is no place to make a stand, old son. Come on, we can drink to what just happened in a safer place."

I said, "I'm new in town," as I turned with my hand out to shake. That was when I got Bama Bob's dumb joke about us being possible kin. The buckskin-clad cuss in a flat Spanish hat who'd just bailed me out was as gray-headed as my grandad but looked more like a Gentleman of Color than any Scotchman *I'd* ever met up with.

He ignored my outstretched hand to say, "To satisfy any questions you'd be too polite to ask, I'd be a maroon, which is the polite Mex term for a runaway nigger."

I nodded soberly and replied, "I don't recall you running away from anyone I care about, and you did say something about having a drink with me, didn't you?"

So he grinned like a big kid and we shook on it as he said, "*Bueno.* I'll explain what I was doing in this copperhead place once I fill you in on where we're going. So let's be going."

I took a step toward the open doorway I'd come in by. The black man in buckskin grabbed my arm and said, "Never go through a bottleneck you just chased an armed enemy through, old son."

I gulped and said, "I follow your drift. The back door, right?"

He shook his head and said, "I'm Jim Beckwourth, the mountain man. I've lived long enough to get famous by never giving nobody the chance to ambush me. There's at least two of them. They know as well as we do that there's two *regular* ways outten here."

Then he drew an awesome bowie knife and added, "It's best we leave irregular. Follow me."

I did, as he strode directly at what seemed to be one blank wall of painted canvas. The barkeep wailed, "Aw, hell, Beckwourth, I wish you wouldn't do that."

I wasn't the only one there who had to chuckle when the black mountain man slashed a man-sized slit in the wall of the saloon and drew one of his dragoon .45s, murmuring, "I'll go first. If I don't get my black ass blown off, feel free to join me out yonder, hear?"

He wasn't shot at, so I followed. We scooted along the narrow slit between the saloon and frame livery, next door, and then we'd made it to even darker surroundings. I had to trust the famous mountain man to lead me through the inky maze and I said so. He laughed and told me this was nothing, next to ducking Mr. Lo on the lone prairie. I asked who Mister Lo was and he asked incredulously, "Ain't you never heard of Lo, the Poor Indian? I thought I heard you say you'd ridden for the Pony Express, old son."

I modestly replied, "Got chased by Shoshone a time or more. But if the truth be known we only lost one rider all the time we carried the mail."

Beckwourth said, "I heard the Pony Express only lasted about a year and a half as a stopgap. You've still had more experience with Mister Lo than a heap of pilgrims out this way. But we'll talk about that later, too. The thing I want you to keep in mind is that the place we're headed is ferociously

Union. That's one of the reasons I'm taking a kid who just got in bad with the Denver Bummers. Are you with me so far?''

I said I was and Beckwourth went on, ''The one thing they were right about, back there, is that nobody loves a mugwump. You got here late for the serious cussing and fussing we had right after we got the news about the slavocrats firing on Fort Sumter last spring. But as you just saw, there's still some dispute as to who's in charge of this spanking new U.S. Territory.''

I said, ''I noticed. But where did all your Deep South Denver boys come from, Colorado being so far north?''

Beckwourth led me through a gap in a board fence and across what seemed to be a lumber yard as he explained, ''There wouldn't be any Denver or even a Camp Cherry Creek, as they called it till just recent, if a mixed party of tame Cherokee and hard-rock miners from Lumpkin County, Georgia, hadn't panned the first color from Cherry Creek, not a quarter-mile from here. You know about the Lumpkin County Strike, of course?''

I had to admit I didn't. Beckwourth swore softly and said, ''I hope you know your alphabet, at least. The first gold anyone ever found north of Old Mexico was panned in the Carolina hills around the turn of this century. The first serious gold rush, before that famous one out Californee way, took place where the Blue Ridge passes through Lumpkin County in the northern hill country of Georgia. The gold they struck there back in Twenty-nine has long been mined entire, of course. But a heap of Georgia boys got a leg up long ago on hard-rock mining and we surely had a lot of Lumpkin County folk in these parts until mighty recent.''

I whistled softly and said, ''I see what you mean about a certain tenseness in the air, out here, when the fighting commenced in earnest back east.''

Beckwourth growled, ''It was a mite too noisy to qualify as just tension. Four days after the *Rocky Mountain News* printed the first word on Fort Sumter, the Denver Bummers run up that Bonnie Blue Flag the South started out with. They flew it from the roof of Wallington and Murphy's, across from where we just now met.''

I whistled again and asked if the two unpleasant gents I'd just had words with might have taken part in that silly business, too.

Beckwourth said he didn't know, explaining, "Most of the original Denver Bummers are long gone. They were led by the ferocious Charley Harrison and another Southron called Captain McKee. He never said what he'd been made captain of. Then there's Sam Logan. Sam's a militia officer now, but during that business he'd gathered an even bigger mob and gave Harrison until sundown to lower his flag and leave it lowered forever-more. For, like it or not, Colorado had just been created a ter-ritory attached to the Union under the Stars and Stripes."

He opened a gate for me on the far side and as we wound up on a dark, cinder-paved side street, he continued, "Lieutenant Colonel William Gilpin, Union Army, arrived just about the same time as the news about Fort Sumter. President Lincoln just appointed us a new civilian governor called Evans. But before that, Gilpin handled them Secesh boys right. He orga-nized us the Denver Guards and Jefferson Rangers and ordered all the gents who didn't want to join the militia to lay down their damned weapons on pain of being forced to *use* 'em, here and now with no more shilly-shally."

I couldn't help asking if the stern governor's orders had applied to bowie knives and dragoon pistols. Jim Beckwourth laughed and said, "Hell, everyone knew them orders didn't apply to us *Union* men, black or white. Charley Harrison knew just who Colonel Gilpin had in mind. Rather than surrender without a fight, or fight a fight he knew he'd never win, Har-rison just gathered together all his Bummers, a hundred or more, and rid out of town under his Bonnie Blue Flag."

There looked to be a dimly lit doorway ahead of us. Beck-wourth said, "That'll be the Jayhawk Saloon. Don't you ever hint you could be a hair undecided when I introduce you as a pal of mine."

I sighed and said, "Bama Bob seems to have made my mind up for me, here in Denver. Where did Harrison, McKee, and all those other pals of Bama Bob head, once they'd been run outten town?"

Beckwourth said, "Most wound up in our Union stockade, where they still languish. Nobody cared where them rebels rode until they robbed some wagon trains and stage coaches. By then the first sort of casual militia outfits had been pasted together as the First Colorado Volunteer Regiment, West Point-style, and issued the cap and balls it might take to deal with a hundred pesky rebels. I am proud to say it was me as scouted Harrison's camp in a sneaky draw and, in the end, the rascals surrendered without a fight."

He waved me through the batwing doors of the Jayhawker and as I stared poker-faced at the regulars, shooting daggers at me with their eyes, Jim Beckwourth stepped in to assure them I was his long-lost love-child from Tennessee. So everyone chuckled and went back to whatever they'd been up to before I had showed up. Jim Beckwourth asked if I'd had supper yet, and when I allowed I'd only chewed some jerky on the trail that afternoon, he set me down at a corner table and rejoined me there a few minutes later with a pitcher of suds, a tray of cold meat, and half a loaf of soda bread.

He let me stuff my face a spell before he said, "I've talked enough about how I got so famous, Ross. Let's hear some more about your time with the Pony Express. I ain't just nosy. I got good reasons for asking."

I rinsed down some headcheese and chewed soda bread before I replied, "I told you and the whole world, before. There's not much to tell. I was having trouble at home with my dad. He couldn't see I'd grown up to where it was for me to decide who I might or might not take to a Sunday-Go-to-Meeting-on-the-Green and, well, I heard they were hiring young skinny kids to carry the mail west from Saint Joe. If the truth be known, I had a tougher time getting out to Saint Joe, Missouri, than I ever had getting from there to Sacramento.

"You see, for each mail run they had all these way stations and we got to change ponies every ten miles or so. Nobody rode more than a hundred miles at a stretch as a rule. Sometimes one of the other boys might be sick or hurt and then you'd have to ride his route, too. But the longest I ever had to go was a tad over three hundred miles in twenty-four hours, with time out to water and grub or take a leak as I was changing mounts. A kid called Pony Bob beat me and even Bill Cody, a riding fool, by streaking almost four hundred miles nonstop.''

Jim Beckwourth lit a long, lean one-cent cheroot and shook out his waterproof Mexican match before he softly observed, ''In sum, you've done some riding in your time, and ain't it true the Pony Express trained you young gents in the fine art of pistoleering?''

I shrugged and said, ''We each got to pack two Colt sixshooters, but nothing heavier. You see, they were charging ten dollars an ounce for the mail we were packing and—''

''You already told us about them laying you off for gaining too many ounces,'' he cut in, insisting, ''tell me about the training they gave you when they issued you them six-guns. Sam Colt created all men equal back in thirty-six. But it's surprising how many gents still favor single-shot this late in the game.''

I said, ''I know. I told you I got chased by Shoshone a time or more. Russell, Majors, and Waddell issued us better mounts to ride as well. The trick was spying Indians before they could head you off. Once it was simply a running gunfight in the open, them with flintlocks on grass-fed ponies—''

''I've outrid some Indians in my time,'' Beckwourth cut in. Then he stared soberly across the table at me and said, ''I want you to answer me dead on the level about this, Ross. Did you ever drop one redskin in your time out there in Indian Country?''

I bit into some more bread, that seeming way more important, and told him, talking with my mouth full, that I'd been paid to carry the mail, not to slaughter savages. I said, ''They tended to drop back as soon as they noticed you lobbing lead their way. I'm sorry I don't have wilder tales to tell about my short career as an old Indian-fighter, Jim.''

He laughed in a deep, mellow way and told me, ''I'm not sorry at all. If you were all bull you'd have bragged on closer calls and more dead Indians than I just heard about. So I suspect you've told me the truth and, in sum, I am talking to a young but not too young gent who knows how to ride, handle a six-gun from the saddle as he's riding, and outwit your average Indian at any distance. What other trades might you have, Ross?''

I swallowed the beer in my mouth and sheepishly allowed, ''I hoe corn well enough but I can't say I like doing it. I never did learn all the tricks of distilling said corn to more valuable produce. Russell, Majors, and Waddell laid me off on the far side of South Pass with winter coming on. I was taken in by a Mormon saddle-maker who let me work for my keep by helping around his shop, just up the delta from Salt Lake City. It wasn't a bad way to get through winter. They treated me decent and the work was sort of interesting.''

Beckwourth asked why I'd left the Mormon Delta, in that case. So I had to allow, ''Sinful habits. Mormons are all right to be around, as long as you don't cotton to tobacco, liquor, tea or coffee. I like all them vices, in moderation, and aside from that they had this young daughter who kept pestering me to join their church so's I could make an honest woman of her once I kissed her.''

Beckwourth nodded understandingly and asked how many times I'd been caught kissing the daughter of the house. I grinned back sheepishly and confessed, ''I never kissed her. I found myself wanting to, a heap. So I lit out before I could wind up a married Mormon saddle-maker who never got to wash his dessert down with even a weak cup of tea. Up around Bitter Creek they told me jobs were opening down here in the Colorado gold fields. So here I am.''

Beckwourth nodded and said, ''So you are. Do you know anything at all about gold-mining, old son?''

I said, ''I didn't know anything about cutting and stitching saddle leather last November. But I was willing to learn, wasn't I?''

He said, ''You might be able to land a job as a mucker, starting at the bottom of the hard-rock trade as well as a mighty muddy hole in the ground. All the easy placer gold's been panned or cradled and it's become a job for professionals, now. You'd do well to make six bits a day as a mucker, Ross.''

I sighed and said that was more than anyone was paying me

right now. He said, "I told you I'd tell you later why I was in that Secesh saloon this evening. This seems to be later. So listen tight. I was there because it's handy to the livery next door and the man I was there to meet would have been riding in from far and wide on a jaded Indian pony. He says his name is John Smith. He says he's lawfully married up with a full-blood daughter of White Antelope. I doubt that, too. But the squaw-man does spend way more time than any other white with the South Cheyenne. As a less-white scout for the Colorado Firsters I have standing orders to keep an eye on the South Cheyenne. Mr. Lo has been acting sort of sassy since most all the regular army troops have been called back east to deal with more obvious dangers to the peace and quiet of this divided land of our'n. How do you like it so far, Ross?"

I frowned in sincere bemusement and replied, "I heard some of the tribes have been acting restless, even for them. I don't see where I fit in, being neither an Indian nor an Indian scout."

Beckwourth said, "That's the job I might be able to get you, Ross. The commander of the Firsters, Colonel Johnny Slough, has close to thirteen hundred men, half of 'em mounted and all decked out with new blue uniforms and mostly modern weaponry. But so far he's only got a handful of *scouts* to keep an eye on Mr. Lo. So how's about it Ross? Indian scouts have the best of both worlds. We get paid better than the poor privates and don't have to go through all that confounded spit and polish. We wears our own duds and never have to peel potatoes, neither. They even lets me drink in the officers' mess, as long as I don't overdo it. But to tell the truth I'd enjoy your company in and about the garrison, old son. Sam Logan and some of the other officers who knew me earlier act friendly enough to me. But some of the younger ones Governor Evans just commissioned seem to take me for some kind of uppity nigger, if you know what I mean."

I said, "I know what you mean. I don't know what they'd make of a Tennessee boy who might have kin riding for the South, for all he knows, by now. Aside from it not being my trade, it ain't my fight until such time as I can be shown for sure which side is right and which is wrong."

He tried, "Hell, Ross. There ain't no Confederate troops to fight out our way. If we fight anyone at all it figures to be Arapaho or South Cheyenne, see?"

I said, "That ain't my fight, neither, knowing as little as I do about either sort of Indian. The only Indians who ever tried to do me a lick of harm were Shoshone and, hell, *they* never *hurt* me. I wasn't brung up to go looking for trouble, thanks just the same. My dad always said, and it's one thing I found I could agree with, that trouble will come looking for you, if only you'll be patient."

Beckwourth said we could still be pals as long as I said I'd think about his offer. So I said I would. But I didn't think, that night, I'd ever wind up scouting for the Colorado Volunteers. That only goes to show how smart my dad was in the end, even if I still say he was a mite too strict.

I wasn't the first and I won't be the last to discover folk don't like to hire you unless you've had some experience, or how tough it can be to get experience when nobody will hire you. I sold my fairly new stock saddle for a pretty good price and got almost as much for the pony, which was costing me way more than I could afford to pay the livery. I had some money left from my last decent job, as well. It ain't fair to call us Scotch folk stingy, but nobody's ever accused us of being *foolish* with our pocket-jingle.

Just the same I came close to starving before I finally landed a job at that tannery just downstream from where Cherry Creek runs into the South Platte.

They said they were willing to teach me the tanning trade if I was willing to work for less than half what a cowhand made, and a cowhand gets his room and board thrown in.

I knew how to ride and shoot but I didn't know how to rope and throw. So mayhaps they *were* fair in paying me what half a cowhand might expect, and it was kind of interesting to learn how to mix all the stinky concoctions it takes to tan different kinds of leather for different purposes. I've never been afraid of hard work as long as I'm told what in thunder to do, and then let me do it my own way at my own pace. So when one of the older hands quit and another with a drinking habit was found in the vats one day, partly tanned and entirely dead, I moved up in seniority and pay a tad.

By that time I'd found a cheap but decent place to board, with a motherly widow woman who changed the bedding every other week and served her boarders second helpings—as long as they meant hash or mashed spuds. So I might well have waited out the war that way if only the infernal war had let me be.

Now that I could afford at least one beer on my way home, and seeing the Jayhawker wasn't too far out of my way, I was able to keep up on old Jim Beckwourth and those Colorado Volunteers he was supposed to be scouting for.

Some of the regulars at the Jayhawkers belonged to the territorial militia. So I soon learned they seemed to have found a mighty soft way to serve with distinction in time of war.

The war being still far off, the one regiment in being and the two still mostly on paper only got together for roll call and a short spell of military drill every Saturday. They were paid for the whole day, even though they met after noon so's most of the troopers could pull the usual half day's Saturday shift at their regular jobs. They got to wear their dapper Union uniforms any evening of the week they liked, and the gals of Denver admired such fighting fools so much that even some of the bummers who'd once followed the Bonnie Blue Flag under Harrison and McKee joined up. Harrison and McKee weren't allowed to, though, even when they said they'd fight Indians for the Union if only Governor Evans would let 'em out of the stockade. There's no record of the governor's reply, if he ever bothered, but as peculiar as it may sound to you, it illustrates the way white folk in the Colorado of that time felt about Indians.

In the golden age Mr. Lo remembered as "The Shining Times" the mountainous half of Colorado Territory had been the happy hunting ground of Shoshone-speaking nations, mostly Ute. The rolling, short-grass plains enclosed in the swamping triangle formed by the North and South Platte Rivers had been the hard core of Arapaho country, with the Arapaho hard and mean as any plains nation who ever rode down a buffalo, or any other likely target for one of their green striped arrows.

North of the Arapaho and hence unimportant to the peace and tranquility of Colorado roamed the fairly friendly Crow and downright testy Lakota, or Sioux.

An Algonquin-speaking nation calling themselves *Tsitsissah*, but known as Cheyenne or "Those who speak funny" to their neighbors, Indian or white, had wound up split into two main groups once they'd been nudged west from their original hunting grounds around the Great Lakes. The North Cheyenne, as George Armstrong Custer found out to his sorrow, allied themselves with the Lakota and took up most of their bad habits. They never amounted to much in Colorado history, either.

The South Cheyenne allied themselves with the Arapaho, or maybe it was the other way round, since long before most of us were on the scene there were way more Cheyenne than Arapaho, mostly hunting from the South Platte to the Kiowa and Comanche haunts south of the Cimarron. Both kinds of Cheyenne liked blue medicine stripes on their arrows. Keep that in mind, because it's important to the way things turned out whilst I was scouting for the Colorado Volunteers.

I wasn't expecting to scout for anybody as I settled into my comfortable rut betwixt the tannery near the river and the boardinghouse near 15th and Wynkoop. From time to time one of the regulars at the Jayhawker would come in with yet another tale of a wagon train missing some oxen or a sassy young redskin shaking a feathered lance at a passing stagecoach from just out of rifle range. But despite ugly tales to the contrary, nobody could name any white in particular who'd lost hair or even a modest amount of blood to the uppity red bastards.

One evening Jim Beckwourth dropped in with that squawman, John Smith, and whilst some of the boys turned up their noses at a black man and a white man who smelt so much like an Indian, I was willing to join 'em when Jim invited me over.

John Smith was a pleasant enough, elderly cuss with a drinker's nose and—there's no nicer way to put it— a disturbing body odor. Now that I know Indians better I must say, to be fair, that they think *we* stink, too. It's not that one breed's all that cleaner than the other. Folk of all colors keep themselves tidy or sloppy, as they see fit. So I reckon it's the food they eat, the soap weeds they wash their duds in, and above all the smoke they so admire that makes Indians smell like . . . let's see . . . dry leaves burning in the fall, with mayhaps some corn husks and at least one cow chip on the pile?

As he drank way more than he et, John Smith told us, in a sort of annoying whinesome way, that we had his in-laws all wrong. I told him I had an open mind about the South Cheyenne, him being about as close as I'd ever got to any, up to now. But he was wound up to defend his father-in-law at the very least and insisted, "Listen, dang it. White Antelope knows better than to tangle with these United States. He's been east to Washington and sports a silver medal President Buchanan gave him, personal. He keeps telling the pinasees the Union is sure to win and not to make the mistake of rising against the whites just because they seem a mite distracted right now."

Jim Beckwourth told me, "Pinasee means warrior." Then he casually asked John Smith, "Who's the chief White Antelope had this interesting discussion with, old Black Kettle?"

The squaw-man looked uncomfortable and said, "Black Kettle's sort of caught in the middle betwixt White Antelope's peace party and, all right, Roman Nose and some of his younger pinasees *have* been sounding off. But I don't see any trouble, this summer, leastways. Bull Bear of the Dog Soldier Society is backing White Antelope's proposal for peace with honor and mayhaps more rations from the Bureau of Indian Affairs. Roman Nose, by himself, hasn't the medicine to sway Black Kettle, and as long as Black Kettle ain't swayed . . ."

"Black Kettle leads the largest band of South Cheyenne," Jim Beckwourth cut in, addressing me. I said I'd heard as much. Jim turned back to the squaw-man and asked, "What about Left Hand, Heap Buffalo, and the other Arapaho leaders, John?"

The other man shrugged and said, "I don't know them as well. There's a couple of lodges of Arapaho hunting with us this summer, but I seem to confuse 'em with my presence and they don't have much to say when I'm about. I can't see the Arapaho rising on their own without the Tsitsissah backing their play. I sure wish you'd pass that on to your blue-belly pals, Jim. You see, my woman's expecting and, well, dang it, I'm right fond of her and her whole band.''

Beckwourth said he felt sure no militiamen with a lick of sense would want to tangle with one more Indian than they really had to. So John Smith got down to serious drinking and that gave me the chance to say I had to be on my way lest I wind up eating a meager portion of cold hash.

Beckwourth said, ''I could fix you up with steak and spuds at least twice a week, Ross. I told you I work six days a week at headquarters as part of the full-time cadre. A junior scout starts at twice the pay of an army private and, like I told you, scouts don't pull kitchen police or interior guard. So what do you say?''

I sighed and said, ''I'd say it sounds tempting as Adam must have found that apple a nekked woman was holding out to him. But I dunno, Jim, I see by the *Rocky Mountain News* that partisan fighting has busted loose back home in Tennessee, with Lord only knowing which side us Clarks are on.''

Beckwourth insisted, ''There's nobody out here for anyone to fight but Mr. Lo, and you just heard John, here, tell you *they* don't aim to rise again.''

I said, ''When I left home they were saying the Dred Scott Decision had settled the argument once and for all and that there'd never be an open break betwixt the North and the South.''

He snorted in disgust. ''The South Cheyenne have no connection with the South that poor Dred Scott tried to get away from. If the Indians stay well behaved there won't be any fighting out our way at all. If they do get uppity, wouldn't you say they *deserved* to have us pals tracking them down for the militia?''

John Smith stared up owlishly from his drink to proclaim, ''Hold on there, darky. There ain't no white scout, or even a black one, as could track Tsitsissah.''

I laughed and said, "I hear you, Mr. Smith. I'm not about to scout for anyone in this-here war."

And that just shows how little we know and how smart we think we are at the age I was, back then.

When my dad had told me all the trouble one man might ever need was as likely to come looking for him as vice versa he'd neglected to add that trouble is one *sneaky* son of a bitch. It knows anyone with a lick of sense tends to ride wide of, say, a couple of Shoshone trying to look innocent down the desert trail ahead, and any man who doesn't decide to go take a leak when the air gets whipcrack-tense in a strange saloon *deserves* that bottle busted over his head.

So, when it happened, it happened with no more warning than a bolt from the blue. It was a sunny Saturday afternoon. I'd just gotten off work at the tannery and, seeing it was so early in the day and I had some pocket-jingle, I was attracted to the spicy aroma wafting my way from a pretty little Mex gal slicing fresh-baked apple pie at a coffee stand facing out onto Wazee Street. The pie smelled pretty good, too. So I ticked my hat brim to her, asked how much they got for a slice, and when she said I could have pie with coffee for a nickel I told her that sounded fair.

She'd just lifted a slice onto a chinaware plate and started to slide it across her counter at me when her sloe eyes got big as saucers and she sobbed, "*Pero no, por favor!*" and so, seeing she couldn't be addressing *me* half that terrified, I naturally rolled along her counter, going for my own gun, as that lion-faced individual I'd had trouble with, way back when, put a bullet through the sheet tin where I'd just been standing. He got off another shot before I could clear my Walker's long barrel from its cross-draw rig, but as we've already established he was not a deep thinker or, it would seem, such a grand shot.

Since folk have always made a sort of legend out of my famous shootout with Bama Bob, the last of the Denver Bummers, I'd best admit, here and now, he'd have had me cold if he hadn't started out to back-shoot me after a whole morning spent at getting drunk. As a beer dray passed behind him, shielding glass and other innocent targets on the far side of the street, I fired. The teamster of the beer dray mistook the intent of all those pistol shots and reined in his team to roll off the far side and run away, yelling for a copper badge to save him and his beer from bandits.

As it was, I hit Bama Bob just below the heart and this slammed him back against the dray. He fell forward to lie with his face in the gutter while a stream of beer from the one keg I'd hulled, along with his chest, made it look like somebody was pissing all over the poor dead cuss. Lord knows who ever wound up with his gun. The copper badges hunted all up and down the bloody, dung- and beer-filled gutter for it, to no avail. They said they needed it as evidence. A couple of other witnesses came forward to back my honest version of the shoot-out. They still said they needed Bama Bob's gun for the cor-oner's inquest, once they peered over the counter and found out the pretty Mex gal had suffered death by gunshot as well.

I don't mind telling you I was mighty worried, even before one of the copper badges asked how come I was packing a six-gun in Downtown Denver to begin with. Still rattled, I pointed at the body sprawled in the gutter to declare, "Good Gawd Almighty! If I hadn't been wearing my own gun I'd be dead as that sweet little gal inside. *She* wasn't wearing no gun when the son of a bitch opened fire and look at all the good that did *her*!"

By this time quite a crowd had gathered, some of it talking ugly about idiots as couldn't leave their war back east where it belonged. Someone else said he'd heard me and Bama Bob were both Secesh, and when one of the copper badges asked me about that I did what you'd have likely done had you been in that fix. I pasted a sincere smile across my numb lips and tried, "Would I be dumb enough to tote a gun for the Con-federacy this opensome? I don't know where the other cuss had *his* gun. The poor little Mex gal who saved me only spotted it at the last."

The narrow-eyed lawman doing most of the asking said he hadn't asked me why Bama Bob had been toting a gun. He wanted to know why *I'd* been toting a gun.

Then one of the onlookers, bless him, called out, "He's all

right, Sarge. He drinks in the Jayhawker with that colored militia scout, Jim Beckwourth.''

The copper badge looked a shade friendlier and said, ''Oh, I see. You must have been on your way to do drill when this back-shooting rebel bastard saw a chance to gun you, away from your militia pals, right?''

I wasn't raised to just plain lie. So I told them that to tell the truth I hadn't joined up yet, but I didn't argue when they assumed I'd meant I was on my way to look into the matter when Bama Bob had seen a chance to settle old scores with me.

So the copper badges told me I was free to go on to militia drill as long as I'd show up for the coroner's hearing whenever they sent for me. When one of 'em warned me not to leave town under any circumstances the older and now friendlier sergeant growled, ''It don't count as contempt of the law as long as a man's called away on military business in time of war.''

Then he glanced from me to the empty space that pretty Mex gal had once sold pie and coffee from, glanced back at me, and softly said, ''If I was an Anglo and I'd been anywhere near a Spanish lady while she was getting shot I reckon I'd *find* me some military business before her menfolk could look me up to discuss the matter with me.''

I protested, ''Hold on, Sarge. I swear on all I hold dear that I had nothing to do with that sweet little gal's death!''

The copper badge shrugged and said, ''I'll buy that, Mr. Clark. There's some, though, who might point out that you were here with her, and that she never would have been shot, by anyone, if you *hadn't* been. Greasers ain't like us, old son. They tend to see things simple. So if I was you I'd go scout Indians or something. Didn't I hear, somewheres, that Black Kettle's band has left the agency again?''

I said I didn't know, but that I might just go looking for 'em, if Jim Beckwourth's offer was still open.

I caught up with Jim amid all the dust and confusion a thousand men and half that many horses and mules stir up by running about in circles. I had to ask a heap of dusty, blue-clad militiamen before I finally spotted Jim Beckwourth's buckskin duds and black face through the drifting clouds of mustard-colored 'dobe dust. As we shook I asked what all the fuss was about and he told me the first regiment was about to march south after a war party someone had reported. When I told him about the fix I was in, he said I was just in time if I wanted to tag along. The colonel had just told them they'd likely be out in the field at least six weeks, and everyone knew it only took a week or so for your average Mex to forget one blood feud in favor of a newer one.

I said I hoped so. He took me by one arm and led me catty-corner across the parade to where some officers were gathered about a map table under the fly of a big canvas tent. Colonel Slough barely looked up when Beckwourth introduced me as the old Indian-fighter who'd saved the Pony Express from the Shoshone and Paiute combined.

The distracted-looking officer just told Jim to get me over to the paymaster and let me sign the standard civilian scout's form. Slough glanced up at me to add, not unkindly, "You'll only draw six bits a day till we see if you're worth even that to us."

Then he shot me a keener look and asked Jim Beckwourth, "Did you just say this lad's an *experienced* scout, Mr. Beckwourth?"

Jim nodded soberly and replied, "He's rid through Indian country alone and come out the far side with all his hair, Colonel. Can half the ribbon clerks and carpenters you've promoted to noncoms in this outfit say the same?"

Slough sighed and, sort of staring through me, said, "All right, Mr. Clark. In addition to your salary as a junior scout you'll draw field rations and fodder for your mount while we're on the trail or in bivouac. As a civilian attached to our regiment for the duration of the campaign you'll be expected to supply your own weapons, mount, and so forth. Are there any questions? Good. We'll be moving out by no later than three. So you'd best get cracking."

I did have some questions. But Jim Beckwourth hauled me off

before I could say so. As he led me through the choking 'dobe dust I protested that I had to give notice at the tannery and that, even worse, I didn't have any damned mount, let alone the saddle, carbine, and possibles that went with the same.

He said it was best to eat any apple one bite at a time, and that he'd signed on as a scout more than once. Money being the root of good as well as evil, he dragged me into the paymaster's tent and got the lance corporal holding down the one field desk to issue me a blank contract. Jim helped me fill it out, since he'd done this chore so many times, but I still got to read it before I signed it and it was sort of interesting the way it worked.

The government enlisted its uniformed help for a fixed three years, if they wanted to be regulars, or the duration of the war plus six months if they wanted to be volunteers. In exchange they got thirteen dollars a month base spending money and were issued all the military kit they'd need along with food and found. Us scouts and other non-military help, such as the regiment surgeon, quartermaster, teamsters, and such, got paid way more and got to quit any time we wanted to with no more punishment than the loss of any back pay we might have coming. After that the soldiers in blue got all the breaks.

The lance corporal let me sign the separate pay book they kept for civilians, but warned me I wouldn't get paid at the end of this particular month. Jim explained they'd make it up to me, next month. So I allowed that sounded fair, even if it did leave me short.

Jim said he'd lend me a double eagle till I did get paid. I said I'd be proud to borrow it, but that I'd never in this world pick up a pony and such other gear as I'd need for any twenty dollars.

He laughed and said, "Hell, old son, I got a whole remuda of riding stock, and don't pay no mind to old Johnny Slough about government issue. Now that we've got you into the fool regiment I'll run you over to meet our battalion commander. We'll be riding with Chivington's battalion, out on point, and you'll find Major Chivington way more interested in making things *work* than pettifogging rules and regulations."

This turned out to be true. Despite what John Smith later said about him at that big hearing, and despite a heap of it being the simple truth, I have to allow that when we first met up, that dusty afternoon, Major John Chivington, as he was then, made a good impression on me.

I didn't know it, as we shook hands across the map table in the First Battalion orderly tent, but the big bluff gent from Ohio was a Methodist minister, well known for his thundersome orations from the pulpit when he wasn't shouting orders one could clearly follow clean across a parade ground or the full length of a military column. Jim told me, later, the major had been the chaplain of an Ohio State Guard outfit before he'd discovered he had a natural call for serious soldiering. I only noticed, at first, what a deep, penetrating voice the fatherly-looking cuss had as he shook with me, man to man, and said of course they'd issue me a cavalry saddle and carbine.

In appearance Chivington reminded me in a nicer way of that rebel cuss I'd just shot it out with. The major was as powerfully built and wore his hair and beard as Bama Bob had. But Chivington's ruddy features were framed by jet-black hair and whiskers, and his flashing eyes peered out from under heavier black brows than most gents grow, or need. I explained to the major I had to tell the tannery I was leaving, lest they waste time searching for me on the bottoms of all them tanning vats, and he agreed it was my Christian duty. He told Jim to ride along with me and make sure I caught up with his battalion if the outfit had moved out by the time we could get back. He smiled at me to explain, "Half our companies are infantry. So we'll not be moving any faster than your average man afoot."

Jim said we'd still best get cracking. The major nodded and told him, "Long as we're drawing Mr. Clark, here, some needed military supplies, you'd better tell the quartermaster I want him to issue you both the same hats and blouses the rest of my boys will be wearing."

Jim Beckwourth looked as surprised as me and replied, "Neither of us are soldiers, Major."

But Chivington insisted. "I don't want anyone mistaking you for a likely target, anyway. You'll be riding in as well as riding out, Mr. Beckwourth, and your point about ribbon clerks was well taken. I want everyone in my command identifiable as such at all times as we march into the great unknown.''

Jim laughed and said, ''Well, we'll gussy-up as pretty as the rest of you if it's free, Major. But, no fooling, do you really think me and Ross look like South Cheyenne, even to a shaky greenhorn?''

Chivington smiled thinly and replied, ''I don't want to worry about that. I've enough on my plate pulling the point position, with most of my men afoot, and nobody issued half the caps and balls we were promised by the infernal War Department. I told you just the hats and blouses would do. Far be it from me to make you give up those greasy fringed pants and ox-blood boots.''

So Jim said he savvied and led me off to confuse me some more. I'm glad I never had to join the regular army—getting attached to the militia is confounding enough.

By the time they had me mounted on a cordovan mare, with a white blaze and stockings and sporting a new cavalry hat and one of them blue, brass-buttoned tunics the quartermaster corps insists on describing as a ''Blouse, General Issue,'' the sun was halfways down the western slope of the sky-bowl and somewhere in the dust some bugler was sounding ''Boots and Saddles.''

I still had to let folks know of my leaving, both at my boardinghouse and the tannery. Jim said, and I agreed, it would save time if we split up and met again in front of the Tremont House where the stage stopped, once I'd gone to the boardinghouse and he'd told them about my quitting at the tannery.

I left my old hat and jacket at the boardinghouse and picked up a few personal luxuries I might have better use for, once my landlady got done weeping all over my new brass buttons and making me promise not to let the savage South Cheyenne take me alive. She said she'd heard they did dreadful things to white captives. She promised to hold my room for me till I got back or she heard I'd been treated dreadful.

I found Jim waiting when I rode on to the Tremont House. He told me they were proud of me at the tannery and that my job there would be waiting if I ever returned from the Indian Wars.

As we rode south together after the outfit, I asked Jim just which band they might be sending us out after. He said, "Can't say for certain. Must be one of the bigger bands if they're talking about six weeks in the field. I'd bet on Roman Nose if I was willing to bet anything on the comings and goings of such undecided sons of bitches. The older chiefs already have their coup feathers, along with plenty of scars. Roman Nose is young and dumb enough to be hankering for hair and glory. He's a mean one, too, even for a crooked-lancer. That's what they call his warrior society, crooked-lancers. You'll see why when we run into 'em."

But we didn't. They hadn't sent us out after Indians at all. I only found out that evening, long after we'd caught up, and it was a mite late to turn back. As we were finishing our supper on the prairie after sundown Major Chivington told us we were marching out to meet a Confederate column coming at us out of Texas. Major Chivington sounded pleased as punch about it, too.

I simmered half the night and stewed about it all through breakfast. By then, through listening to the officers jawing about it, I had a better notion as to what in blue blazes was going on. It was good to know that Jim Beckwourth hadn't been acting cute with me, at least. He hadn't known, any more than anyone else below the rank of a field-grade officer, because they'd sent us south under sealed orders. You may recall what I've already told you about some old boys who'd started out Secesh joining the Colorado Volunteers, and you think *I* was pissed?

When a delegation of such boys approached the major to explain they'd only signed up to fight Indians and that they'd be damned if they'd fight other Southrons, the preaching militant just smiled at them in a fatherly way and declared, loud and clear, "We don't *damn* deserters in this man's army. We hang 'em high, from a wagon tongue if no tree is handy."

Once he saw he had their undivided attention he added, not

unkindly, "You men will follow orders until such time as you may be executed for misbehavior before the enemy, killed by the enemy, or return to Denver victorious to be mustered out in Our Lord's good time."

One of 'em, a corporal from Georgia, managed to say, "But, major . . ." and then John Chivington was up atop an ammunition box, his cavalry saber flashing above his head in the early morning light as he thundered, "Attend my words, all of you! It was not *we* who rent our Glorious Union asunder with this dire Civil War! It was the villainous slavocrats who decreed our house divided, just because they were born too lazy to pick their own cotton and too cheap to pay anyone *else* to do it! Was it *we* who fired on Fort Sumter? It was not! Is it *we* marching up out of Texas to seize the Colorado gold fields for the Confederacy? It is not! Hear ye, hear me one and all, just as Adam sinned in The Garden of his own free will, so did those black-hearted sinners fire on the very flag of their own country. And let this be our answer to them, down through all the ages. . . ."

Then he started singing. I'd heard the hymn he was singing before, albeit I'd never paid much attention to the words. But now, out there on the prairie with the dew still shining on the tawny buffalo grass as if the world was getting born anew I heard other militia men around me singing along with the major, some moving closer, with tears in their fool eyes, as he roared out like some sort of singing lion:

> Mine eyes have seen the Glory of the coming of The Lord!
> He is tramping out the vintage where the grapes of wrath are stored!
> He's unleashed the fateful lightning and his terrible swift sword. . . .

It takes more than even a good marching song to convince a Tennessee boy. What convinced me most was my feet. Jim and me had caught up with the Colorado First a good ways south of Denver after considerable riding. I didn't own the pony I'd ridden so far from home on. Getting back to town afoot figured to be chore enough, without all those other Firsters commenting on it, or worse, if I had to file back along the long column after stripping off my hat and uniform blouse.

On the other hand, the longer I stuck it out, the farther I'd be from anywheres I wanted to be when things really got stuck in my craw. I explained this to Jim when he joined me, squatting morose by a dying fire, well after "Boots and Saddles" had sounded.

He said, "I follow your drift, and I can see how you'd have less against the Confederacy than a gent of my complexion, Ross. But let's study on who we're riding out to meet and what you'll be called upon to do about it, if we meet 'em."

I insisted, stubbornly, "I don't want to aim gun-one at anyone from the South, lest he turn out kin."

"To begin with, us scouts ain't expected to shoot *nobody*. Our job is to spot the other side's position and get back to our side without anyone noticing they've been spotted."

I shook my head and said, "Pointing a man out for someone else to shoot ain't all that different than shooting him personal, is it?"

Beckwourth said, "I can see you ain't shot many men. Be that as it may, I can promise you no Tennessee boys will be with the Texas trash of Sibley's so-called Confederate Brigade. Saddle up and I'll tell you what I know about General Henry H. Sibley of San Antone and his West Texas Volunteers."

Naturally Jim's bay gelding was saddled up and ready to move out. As he helped me saddle my own pony Jim said, "For openers, old Hank Sibley's no more a general of anything than you are. Him and his command are guerrillas, operating on their own."

I couldn't help asking, "You mean like us?"

To which he replied with a scowl, "Bite your tongue. Our officers hold proper commissions, signed by Military Governor Gilpin and confirmed by that new civilian cuss, Evans, with the full approval of the Union War Department in Washington. Make sure you get that cinch tight, Ross. This old bitch-pony has a peculiar sense of humor."

I kneed the cordovan to deflate her swollen girth and pull the cinch leathers tighter as Jim went on, "I'll grant you Robert E.

Lee and even J. B. Hood, in command of the *uniformed* Texas troops, can qualify as real soldiers if you'll allow Sibley and his ragged-ass irregulars can't. Sibley *says* he's gathered together a mess of Texas trash to seize the gold of the West for the Confederate Cause. It might be interesting to see how much gold he'd pass on to the Montgomery Mint if he won. But he ain't about to win and—Do Jesus, ain't you ready *yet*, old son?''

I swung myself up aboard my pony and asked him why he was still goldbricking on his feet in a deserted camp. So he laughed, mounted up, and we lit out at a lope for the head of the column.

Since you can't carry on much of a conversation at a lope or even a trot I got to ponder what he'd just told me as we overtook the point. That took longer than it takes to just say so. Aside from the 1,342 fighting men and attached civilians, Colonel Slough was leading a considerable number of wagons, from ammo to chuck, with the men in column-of-fours, whether mounted or afoot, and the wagons Indian-file along the dusty trail we were following across the rolling prairie. But, being we got to lope, we finally overtook the fluttering guidons of Chivington's battalion, in the lead. As he spotted us, Major Chivington waved us on, shouting something about knowing where he'd just been and wanting to damn it know where he was *going*.

Jim led me on until we seemed to have the sea of grass all to ourselves before he reined in, saying, ''All right, we'd best start to teach you how a scout earns his keep. The other junior scouts, out to the flanks, already know their ropes. You'd best ride tight with me at least as far as Raton Pass. By then you ought to have some notion as to what you're doing and, if you don't, I won't want such a fool riding with me in enemy country!''

I said, ''Hold on, Jim. I ain't said, yet, who the enemy of me and mine might be. It's all very well for you to describe the boys we're riding agin as bandits, but ain't this a mighty serious posse to send after bandits?''

Beckwourth laughed and replied, ''Depends on how big a

gang of such border ruffians old Sibley has assembled. All I could get from Colonel Slough this morning was unconfirmed. Military Intelligence, which is polite for Yankee spies along the Rio Grande, puts Sibley's so called West Texas Brigade at around three thousand.''

I whistled, and glanced back the way we'd just ridden to see nothing but a faint haze of dust along the horizon. "That'd have us outnumbered better than two to one, right?''

Jim shrugged and said, "Look on the bright side. They say Sibley's hauling a couple of batteries of field artillery after him. That ought to slow him down and limit his chess moves if we can beat him into the mountains of New Mexico.''

I sighed and said, "Damn it, Jim. I ain't even said I'm in this to the end, and you're already making me look yellow-bellied if I pull out now. What kind of a chicken-liver would excuse himself from a fight, with any fool excuse, once he'd been told it would be an uphill fight against such dire odds as you just mentioned?''

Jim said, "He'd surely have to be yellow-bellied. But, like I said, your odds of crossing swords with any Tennessee boys are mighty slim.''

I said, "I ain't packing no sword. What are my odds on coming out of this fight with Texas trash alive?''

Jim Beckwourth smiled thinly and said, "Oh, I'd say they'd be mighty slim, too. But what do you want, egg in your beer?''

And so I decided to stick it out until such time as I met up with a known blood relation dressed in butternut gray. It wasn't as easy as it sounds. Colonel Slough set a killing pace, albeit only horses and mules really died or had to be shot along that long dusty trail across all them awful miles of nothing much.

It was bad enough out on point, where we rode, for we had to press our ponies hard to keep far enough ahead to matter. It seemed we'd no sooner rein in on some high rise for a good keen look around before we'd spy Chivington's red-and-white guidons fluttering over the horizon at us and have to push on, hoping for the best.

Despite what old Jim had said about ribbon clerks, the Col-

orado Firsters were good. Militia or not, they marched fast or
faster than most Union regulars could have been expected to.
The fact that they were all volunteers—the Union draft hadn't
started yet—meant no sissy-boys had joined up to begin with.
A good many of them *were* ribbon clerks, or Denver clerks, at
any rate, but most had been tested by the very fact they'd
chosen to seek their fortunes way out west. The first generation
actually *born* in Colorado hadn't learned to walk good enough
to march with the Colorado Volunteers and, of the three Colorado regiments, the Firsters were the best trained and tough-
est.

As I got to know them, in camp some evenings when it
wasn't my turn to be way out on the prairie as a night picket,
I learned our Major Chivington had sort of skimmed the cream
of the cream. Colonel Slough was boss of the whole regiment,
but Major Chivington had a way with words as well as a
stubborn streak. He'd gone through all the records of all the
officers and men in the regiment and thrown his weight to shift
a man here and pick up an extra mount there till he had mostly
former buffalo-hunters, cowhands, and hard-rock miners, or at
least farm boys who could keep going no matter how long and
hot a day seemed to be shaping up. He had half of his four
hundred dragoons, as he called 'em, mounted. Dragoons are
soldiers who ride to meet the enemy on horseback and then
dismount to fight as riflemen on foot. So he had his men take
turns riding and walking every other day. That way everyone
got practical experience at both a dragoon's chores, and no
doubt the major paid attention to which officers and men were
the best.

I didn't get to know the other civilian scouts attached to the
Firsters as well as I got to know Jim Beckwourth. It wouldn't
have been polite to horn in when they reported in to Jim as their
senior from time to time. They mostly reported to the commissioned officers they were assigned to. I can recall a few of
the scouts. I know one was black as Jim, but passing himself
off as a Seminole from the Indian Nation. Another looked more
Indian to me and allowed he was a Pawnee breed. The other
old boys have become more blurred to me, in their dusty

buckskins and hickory shirts. Only Jim and me, scouting for Chivington, were required to wear military hats and blouses.

In the end this turned out sort of smart, after all. I'd just been allowed to ride alone, off to Jim's flank so's we could cover more of the unknown swells and draws ahead, when I discovered how much I still had to learn. I hadn't spotted that diamond patrol of boys in blue until I came over a rise at 'em, and they'd have nailed me for certain if they hadn't noticed I was wearing the same Yankee Blue.

They were patrolling out of Fort Wise, a prairie outpost made of mostly sod. I told 'em I was looking for their fool fort and acted as if they hadn't scared me out of a year's growth. So they said they'd be proud to ride back to the main column with me and guide us fool irregulars to safety before nightfall caught us on the lone prairie.

That was only the beginning. We were supposed to hole up at Fort Wise and await further orders. The regulars soon discovered just how disorderly the volunteers could get when anyone implied they were less worthy of respect than any other son of a bitch in this man's army. So after a dozen fistfights and one ugly knifing they let us camp outside the walls and protect the sissy regulars from coyotes, jack rabbits, and such.

Then word came over the telegraph wires, confirming that Sibley's brigade really had that artillery, mountain howitzers lobbing cannister shot and bomb shells. Worse yet, they'd moved up into New Mexico Territory within sight of the Sangre de Cristos without meeting enthusiasm or resistance from the mostly bemused Mex population. So we were on the march some more, at such a killing pace we got to Trinidad with less'n half the four-legged stock we'd started out with.

The army remount service at Trinidad fitted us with mounts and pack animals—the poor critters—for our Colonel Slough had heard other Colorado troops, two companies made up in part from the old Guards and Rangers, had beat us to Santa Fe, to make a stand there with a Colonel Canby and his U.S. Army regulars.

Not wanting to miss out on the hoedown, we bulled over Raton Pass and made a forced march to Fort Union, New

Mexico, where even Johnny Slough allowed a few day's rest wouldn't kill any of us.

At this point it was still our nominal commanding officer who was full of piss and vinegar. Considering what many would say about him later, with good reason, John Chivington showed uncommon common sense when word came over the wire that things were surely going to pot just over the Sangre de Cristos to our west.

Slough and most of the others wanted to mount up and ride on to Victory or Death when they heard Sibley's tough Texans had sliced through Canby's lines like a hot bowie knife through butter and that Santa Fe had fallen, with all the Union forces south of us killed, captured, or scattered from hell to breakfast!

As a scout, I got to hang around the map tables more than your average enlisted trooper. So I was there when Major Chivington said, or preached, it was hard to say which; "They promised they'd send the caps we're still short of to Fort Wise. If they did, the shipment never caught up. They promised the caps would be waiting for us at Trinidad. Then they said they'd get them *here*, instead, by mule express through the mountains. My men are still waiting. We've powder and ball for mayhaps one fine fight. But you can't fire one ball without one cap and, as of last inspection, my men are packing less than a dozen caps apiece!"

A junior officer said, "If the major will permit, four hundred men firing a dozen times adds up to quite a fusillade, to me."

Chivington snorted in disgust and replied, "I can see you haven't been to see the elephant yet, mister. I haven't marched my brave boys all this way to see them slaughtered like sheep by the godless Texas slavocrats! Sibley already has us outnumbered. Do we propose to give him the lives of our brave lads on a silver platter by sending them into battle with no way to fire back? The black-hearted spawn of Satan have just licked Union Regulars who *had* guns that fired, for the love of God!"

Then he stormed out of Colonel Slough's quarters as if overcome by emotion. So he never had to answer when that same junior officer wondered, softly but out loud, where the military genius might have been in a battle before.

Some of them laughed. But Captain Logan, the one who'd led the Denver Stranglers, or Vigilance Committee, before the war had become so formal, growled, "He may be a mite flamboyant but he's still right. If Sibley's holding Santa Fe it means mean and dirty, house to house and over 'dobe walls. He's going to be a bitch to pry out of there, even if we had twice his strength and ten times as much ammunition. Since we don't, I vote we dig in here at For Union until either those caps and some reinforcements arrive from the north or Sibley moves on us from the west. Sooner or later both have to happen. Let's just hope our caps get here first, and a couple of howitzers for outside would sure come in handy, come to study on it."

A couple of other officers voted to hold Fort Union against all comers. Colonel Slough raised a hand for silence. "This military unit happens to be the First Colorado Volunteers, not a budding democracy, and I'll remind you gents that I'm in command of the same. So here's what we're going to do. We're going to wait no more than ten days for those blasted caps, more riding stock, and let's hope more men. But then, come hell or high water, I mean to march on Santa Fe and take it back for the Union!"

Logan insisted, "Colonel, you don't *have* to march out from ahint these swell walls to get at old Hank Sibley. Them rebels are out to grab the gold fields of Colorado, and to do so they have to come through this-here fort because it guards the only decent wagon trace through Raton Pass!"

Another company commander nodded in agreement and said, "We've men enough to hold this fine fort against all comers, just as Travis held the Alamo against that way bigger army, Colonel."

John Slough cocked an eyebrow across the map table at the optimist and quietly replied, "Bullshit. That's all the fight at the Alamo ever was. If Travis had known beans about basic military tactics he'd have never allowed his pitiful handful of irregulars to die so dumb. By holing up behind mud walls that way, Travis and his people gave themselves to the Mexicans on the silver platter Major Chivington just mentioned. When you know your enemy has you outnumbered and outgunned you meet him out in the field, where he can't surround you and whittle you down at his leisure. Santa Anna was advancing on San Antone with artillery that time, too, come to study on it. So it was mighty dumb of Travis to take all his people to church and watch 'em die, within two pathetical weeks! So, like I said, gentlemen. With or without all the tools of the trade we might want, we're going out to fight them sons of bitches in the field, like the soldiers we're supposed to be, damn it!''

We marched out of Fort Union the morning our colonel had said we ought to. Our men and the stock we had left were well rested and we'd even picked up a few more men and their mounts. The survivors of both Canby's defeat and the fall of Santa Fe had to get out of them parts by way of Raton Pass. While a heap of 'em skirted Fort Union and just kept going, having had their fill of the war, others joined up with the Firsters, spoiling for another crack at Johnny Reb.

Best of all, a couple of mule loads of percussion caps and even more powder and ball caught up with us at last. This made Major Chivington a heap more popular with both the officers and men, seeing it had been his grand notion to wait up for those caps, and oh how good it felt to have a cap for every waxed-paper cartridge in your belt cases. It was likely the good advice he'd already imparted had persuaded Colonel Slough to give Chivington a mite more slack on the reins than he seemed to give his other officers. I wasn't invited to the argument, but since I took part in the results I'd say the major sold the colonel on the commonsense notion that four hundred men could move faster on horseback than both riding and walking. I was there, with Jim, when Slough gave us our final instructions before cutting us loose to fan way out ahead of the main outfit, all mounted.

Fort Union was set in a raggedy wrinkle the Pecos run down. Santa Fe was in the north-south fold of the upper Rio Grande. So, in sum, we had us a complexicated crumple of sandstone ridges—the Sangre de Cristos—betwixt our main columns. We knew Sibley would want to work his way east through the mountains to take Fort Union and the trail from there north to the Colorado gold country. If we wanted to take Santa Fe back we had to work our way west. Whichever side spotted the other first would be in a swell position to ambush it. Two armies feeling one another out works a heap like Hide and Seek, save for being way more lethal on the losers.

Most of the time we had to rely on sheer guesswork. Riding through all those twisty silent canyons from Fort Union, never knowing what you'd see around the next bend—first, if you were lucky—I gained a first-hand knowledge of why army commanders since the time of Joshua have sent scouts out ahead as they were creeping into the Promised Land.

Jim Beckwourth did as well by Major Chivington, the first day out, as Caleb did by Joshua in the Good Book. It was me who heard cows lowing somewheres ahead, reined in to dismount in some sticker-bush, and scrambled up atop some rim rock for a look-see. But I wasn't sure what I was seeing before old Jim eased up beside me, muttering, "Take off that fool hat when you're staring down with sky ahint your head, old son. What have we yonder?"

I told him to see for himself. We were both staring down into the same sweet little mountain glen, watered by a shallow creek winding through cottonwood and black willow. The cows I'd heard numbered at least three score. There were some goats browsing along the creek as well. The ranch house was low-slung and 'dobe-walled, with a sod roof. The whitewashed crapper out back made me consider Anglo ownership. The chicken coop was whitewashed, too. There was a goodly number of ponies to count, tethered in the dooryard or pent in the corral to one side. I said so. Jim Beckwourth said, "Never mind the ponies. Look at all them *saddles*!"

So I did, felt my ears burn a mite, and said, "Lord, I'm dumb. You're right, Jim. No way in hell a cattle spread as small as that would carry such a grand remuda and, even if they did decide to raise horseflesh instead of beef, there's no place down yonder for that many riders to *bunk* regular."

Jim nodded soberly and said, "I make it a score of saddle horns I can plainly see. Lord knows how that one ranch house has room for all them visiting riders, but here's what we'd best do about 'em. I want you to get back to the major. Tell him what we've found here, so far, and see what he wants to do about it. I'll stay here and keep an eye on 'em. The sun ball's high and hot. I doubt they'll move on before you can get back here with the others, if you start right now. So what are you waiting for?''

I slid back down the rocks a heap faster than I'd come up and it only took make a few minutes to bump into Major Chivington in a canyon. He was further along it than he was supposed to be before Jim and me had finished scouting it. When I told him what we'd found he acted smart enough, though. He made me dismount and draw him the best map I could manage in the dust. Then he told one of his company commanders to move on down and cover the mouth of this canyon, near Jim's lookout. He asked how come I was still on my feet and, as soon as I got back in the saddle, he ordered me to find him and his three other companies a way round to the south of the ranch. When I confessed I hadn't the least notion as to how these blamed hills had been carved by the Good Lord's patient wind and water he said I'd best find out soon as possible, since the morning was almost shot and this canyon maze figured to get hotter before it got cooler.

So I did it. The telling in detail would be even more tedious than the long, twisty ride, with more than one dead-ended box canyon to turn back from. But an hour or more had us south of the ranch house and the tree-lined creek.

Major Chivington had everyone dismount and spread out in a mighty long skirmish line. Three hundred dragoons may not sound like all that many on paper, but spread ten feet apart and coming through dry grass and wild mustard at you, with carbines capped and cocked at port arms, they must look mighty ominous. For just about the time we were set to ford the creek the rebs inside the house sent a Pigeon out to ask our terms.

I'd best explain, since lots of folk still laugh when they hear mention of events at the Pigeon ranch, that Pigeon was the family name of the Anglo family who raised beef there, with the help of some Mex *vaqueros* and all the *mujeres* and *muchachacallits* as go with such prolific breeders.

The Pigeon kid who'd come out to us told Major Chivington there were indeed twenty Texans holed up inside, a couple of 'em heat-stroked and all of 'em mighty worried right now. Being New Mexico mugwumps, the Pigeons hadn't cared who might win until just now. The kid said he felt sure his folk would just as soon see the last of the loud-mouthed free-loaders from Sibley's brigade. So Chivington told the kid to go back and say they had five minutes to surrender or be blown to Kingdom Come by our long-range field guns, back up the slope.

That sent the kid running. I couldn't help asking the major when and where we'd wound up with our own artillery. He just laughed and told me fibs didn't count as sins in time of war.

That particular whopper surely worked. In less than five minutes a score of hangdog Texas Volunteers filed out of the Pigeon house, proceeded by a white pillowcase on a broom handle. Major Chivington had our boys disarm 'em and line 'em up on the sunny side of the house. Then he looked the whole ragged-ass lot of them over, from back aboard his cavalry charger, and informed them as if from the pulpit, "You men have been taken in arms behind Union lines in civilian costume. Under the Articles of War that gives me every right to execute you posthaste as partisans. I don't have the bullets to spare for the usual firing squads but, as you may have noticed, there are plenty of stout trees along yonder creek. So now we'd best commence separating the sheep from the goats."

An older rebel who might have been in command at one time called out, "Hold on there, Yankee! Me and the boys ain't part of nothing. We're the advance guard of Scurry's column, sent out by General Sibley to take that pesky Fort Union afore you Yanks could reinforce it."

Chivington chuckled fondly and said, "Your colonel left Santa Fe a little late. How do you distinguish officers from the rest of your rabble, since you all seem to feel this war's a cattle drive?"

The Texican in the work duds of a cowhand shrugged and said, "We manage. General Sibley and some of the staff officers do have uniforms. Uniform blouses, leastways. They say we'll all get fitted out like regulars, once we capture all that gold for our side."

Chivington smiled thinly and said, "Meanwhile we seem to have captured you, and as I just informed you, I have every right to hang you as the cur dogs you appear to be."

More than one worried rebel protested he was no damned cur dog. So Chivington said we'd see about that. Then he dismounted, went inside, and once he'd paid his respects to the lady of the house and been seated at her kitchen table with some of the swell coffee she'd been brewing for Texas, Chivington had the Texans led in to him, one by one. As he got each alone he told them the same thing. He said that every one of them would have the same opportunity to come clean about the disposition of their main column, with no chance to compare stories with a fellow prisoner. Those prisoners whose stories agreed with the majority would be spared. Those who seemed to be lying would be hanged that very day from the nearest tree.

I was there, so I can tell you this democratic way of separating the truthsome sheep from the lying goats sure works swell when the gent with power of life and death over you is a big growly cuss with a bushy black beard and eyes that glow like coals.

We had this one lance corporal, we called him Four Eyes, who worked as a draftsman in Denver when he wasn't pulling militia duty. So even though the one ordinance map we had of those parts was way off, Four Eyes and the major began to put together a way better one with the help of the Pigeons and scared prisoners, all of whom knew way more than any government survey team ever had.

I don't know what Chivington did with the very few Texas riders who told him to go to hell. I had to leave right off when the major called me over to the table, handed me a penciled tracing of the map he and Four Eyes had just laid out, and told me to pick out a fresh mount from the Pigeon remuda and get back to Colonel Slough with the news on the double. As I folded the paper and put it away he added, "Tell Slough I'm advancing on this Scurry and his scum from here, within the hour, and—"

"Begging the major's pardon," I cut in, "didn't Colonel

Slough tell us not to engage the enemy if we could help it, before he caught up?''

Chivington snapped, "Pay attention, Clark! It can't be helped. The prisoners tell me Scurry's column is winding its way up through the canyonlands just south of here, spread out like the irregulars they are. I don't want to give them the chance to bunch up as they may at nightfall. There's a Major Pyron, Charles S. Pyron, not far from here with the battery of mountain howitzers we heard about. Tell Slough I don't mean to attack the main rebel column, just Pyron's artillery. Get a move on, son. The colonel will know how important it is to capture those enemy field guns!''

I got a move on. A friendly *vaquero* picked out a good Spanish riding mule for me and helped me saddle the same. I must have looked sort of comical as I loped north aboard that lop-eared wonder, but it sure could move. And the best thing about riding mules in semi-desert country is that they get by on way less water than any horse. That's how come the Butterfield Stage always used mules through Apacheria, the way they run.

I passed Jim Beckwourth and the reserve company and waved them on to the Pigeon ranch, the way the major wanted me to. All this while, of course, Colonel Slough and our main column had been poking along at an infantry pace. So I never had to ride all the way back to where we'd started, that morning. Our part-Pawnee scout spotted me first, coming in. So it was a good thing the major had had made me wear the Union hat and blouse after all. The breed took me up a side canyon, where the outfit had just fallen out for their noon meal. Colonel Slough talked nice to me until he figured out what I was saying. Then his face clouded over and he jumped up from his camp table, roaring, "Thunderation and Lord Gawd! What does Chivington think he's doing?''

I said, "Attacking them Texans, he says, sir. He said it seemed best to hit 'em piecemeal, whilst they're spread out, like us.''

Slough called to his bugler, "Sound Assembly! We've got to catch up with that blithering preacher before he leads four hundred of my best men directly into the Great Beyond! If

they're calling that Scurry rascal a *colonel* it means he's leading at least a *regiment*, not a battalion, like Chivington's!"

I said, "I think he knows that, Colonel. He never said he
aimed to attack that Colonel Scurry's main party. Just that
other major, out to one side with them howitzers."

Slough went on cussing as the regiment broke camp. I
soothed, "The major took the Pigeon ranch smooth as silk, and
won't it be an even-numbers fight, Chivington's battalion
against Pyron's?"

Slough sobbed, "Jesus H. Christ! You just said Pyron has
mountain howitzers as well as all the mountains he may ever
need to set them up in. The book says you never attack in even
numbers, even when you have the enemy out in the open. The
advantage is always with the side on the defensive. Didn't you
know that?"

I said, "I do now, sir. I suspicion Major Chivington may
not, or may not care if he does."

It can take forever to get a military column moving again. So
long before he could, Colonel Slough had me riding back to
Major Chivington with his own direct orders. Chivington was
to wait up for Slough at the Pigeon ranch or, if he'd already
left, get his dumb ass back there *poco tiempo*. Under no circumstances was he to advance another step down the primrose
path to perdition.

Passing such orders on was easier said than done. When I
got back to the ranch I found the place held by no more than
a platoon, left behind to guard those prisoners and make sure
the Pigeons stayed on our side and didn't ride off anywheres to
tell tales out of school.

I changed mounts again, lashed some extra canteens to my
saddle, and rode along the wagon trace they said the major and
the rest of the boys had taken.

I hadn't ridden far before I heard what I took for distant
thunder, till I noticed how cloudless the cobalt sky above me
was. So, seeing that the wagon trace trended away from the
sounds of the battle, I cut through the high chaparral over hill
and dale till I was considerably lost, save for the crackle of

small arms and the occasional *crump* of a howitzer to assure
me that wherever the hell I was, I was surely mixed up in a
battle.

Since the mighty confusing afternoon near the Pigeon ranch
I've had heaps of time to study the maps they drew up, later,
to explain all our confusion. It makes mayhaps a mite more
sense on paper, with neat blue lines showing where we were
under Chivington and neat red lines indicating Pyron's positions. A real firefight, however, don't look half so neat when
you're taking part in it.

What I recall the most about the hot, dry afternoon is the
smell. Northern New Mexico is covered with a mostly ever-
green mixture of tall scrub and runty trees they call high chaparral. When you bust it up, whether by chasing a cow or
lobbing a cannon ball through it, it smells like the medicine
you rub on your chest when you've got the croup. So see if you
can imagine the nose-tingles inspired by chest salve, gunsmoke, dry drifting dust, and horse shit, all at once.

I passed one dead horse with its guts spilt open and stinking
bad already before it occurred to me I'd best dismount and lead
my mule afoot. The brush about us was saddle-horn high,
enough to hide us, even if it wasn't bulletproof. The mule
didn't cotton to the notion of coming along with me, as I
advanced on the loudest gunfire. I jerked the bit cruel, to let it
know I could be as stubborn, and said, "I know this looks
foolish, mule. But we got to get to Major Chivington, and if he
wasn't in the middle of all this noise it wouldn't be so noisy,
hear?"

A few yards on I saw what had spooked the poor dumb
brute. A blue-clad figure was crawling ahead of us in the
chaparral, leaving a dotted line of fresh blood spatters in the
powdery dry dust behind him. I figured he'd started out aboard
the gut-shot horse back yonder. As he heard us overtaking him
he rolled on his back to cover his scared face with a dusty
forearm, pleading, "Don't shoot me again! I'm already hit and
I surrender, see?"

I recognized him, now, as that kid who worked in a drugstore near 17th Street when he wasn't playing Soldier Blue. I

took one of the canteens from my mule and hunkered down beside him, saying, "I'm Ross Clark, one of your scouts, you sorry sight. Where are you hit?"

He took the canteen from me and would have guzzled the whole gallon in one gulp if I'd let him. When I didn't he blessed me anyways and said, "I aint sure if I'm hit or if I busted something when they sent all that grape through my pony. Either way, I can't get either leg to work no more. I feels all pins and needles from my belt-line down."

I hung the canteen on a scrub pine bough and gingerly examined him for punctures, as I asked what on earth had been going on around here. He told me he'd found it mighty confusing, too, when old Major Chivington had suddenly whipped out a sword and ordered his bugler to sound the charge. The injured drugstore clerk said, "I was charging before I saw who we was charging at. Then some bastards I never saw fired off this swamping gun I only recall as a barn-sized white puff, and the next thing I knew . . . Do you reckon I'm done for, Clark?"

I told him he didn't seem to be busted open and tried to convince him he'd only had the wind knocked out of him. He said, "I think I've been bleeding out my ass." I didn't argue. He was in a better position to know. He was surely bleeding somewhere, even though I couldn't find any torn-open parts to his damp and sticky pants. I told him I had to catch up with the major and asked him, again, to give me some damned indication as to where all the others might *be* right now. He insisted I knew as much as he did.

Then another voice called out, in a surprisingly conversational tone, "Say, Yankee, could you spare a dying man just a swaller of that water?"

After the hairs on the back of my neck settled back down I saw that yet another old boy had been lying there, almost in plain sight, all the time. Only he was wearing gray pants, a sort of burlap-colored shirt, and had so much trail dust all over him that he'd sort of blended into the dappled shade of the rabbit bush he lay sprawled in.

I figured he'd had plenty of time to gun me, had he still wanted to continue the war in this part of the battlefield. So I crawled over to him with the canteen, saying, "Sip this slow till we see if you're gut-shot, Tex."

He took the canteen, gulped thrice, and held it back up to me as he lay back with a wistful smile, murmuring, "I must be. I'm still thirsty but it hurts to swallow. You boys must be that famous Iron Brigade we've heard so much about. The damn fools tolt us we had only a handful of regular army and some sissy militia to worry about betwixt Santa Fe and Pikes Peak. Who's that devil incarnate with the bushy hair and black beard, Attila the Hun?"

I chuckled down at him and said, "He only thinks he is. I'm trying to catch up to the cuss with orders to pull back, Tex. Might you have any notion where they're holding the dance right now?"

The badly wounded guerrilla coughed, spraying both of us with bitty flecks of blood, and said, "As long as any of our boys are still able, they'll never run off from our field guns. We never hauled 'em all this way to hand over to you Yankees."

I insisted, "I'm not out to capture your artillery, Tex. I only want to find our own CO!"

The dying boy muttered, "He's the one trying to capture our field guns, damn it. He's been chasing our artillery all over this damned valley like a goddamn cat chasing a mouse around the kitchen! Ain't you got ears?"

I cocked my head to listen sharper. As I heard the deep-throated cough of a howitzer just about due south of us, I said so. The Texan didn't answer. It took me a few stunned seconds to make sure he was really dead, the way he was staring at me with that soft little smile on his pale lips.

The boy in blue was dead by this time, too. He'd just drifted away while I'd been talking to our mutual and now former enemy. I regathered the mule's reins and forged onward toward the rumble of the main engagement. I knew we were getting closer when we passed more men, mounts and scrub pines cut down by shot and shell. We topped a gentle rise and now I had a better view of the proceedings as I gazed down into the wide shallow draw ahead. Those big white puffs the dying drugstore clerk had mentioned were sprouting all along the far crest. There seemed to be about seven big guns firing my way. Figuring eight to a battery, that meant one had been captured or put out of commission. I couldn't see the ragtag rebs that'd be lined up in the chaparral this side of their howitzers. But once I spotted the first flash of blue against the spinach-green and mustard dust down yonder I saw that most of Chivington's four hundred were still in action, advancing in skirmish lines afoot, with one man in each squad holding their mounts to their rear. I'd just spotted Chivington's bulky blue form and the buckskin pants of old Jim Beckwourth when a bugle sounded "Boots and Saddles." I figured it had to be a Texan acting cute. Nobody in his right mind would order his men to mount and charge uphill into artillery fire.

Only, within minutes, that's just what that crazy, or foxy, Major Chivington had them do! I couldn't believe my eyes. Some of those Texans across the way must have thought they were seeing things, too, as John Chivington charged straight at them, firing six-guns with both hands and yelling like a banshee squatting on a buzz saw!

One rider, however fearsome, might not have cowed a whole battalion of anybody. But as Chivington rode through shot and shell as if encased in invisible armor, the rest of his followers came tearing after him in a flying wedge of cussing and shooting determination. So while some of the Colorado boys who'd begun the charge with Major Chivington never made it to the enemy guns, enough did to capture the same, as their gun crews joined the other Texas guerrillas in the general retreat over the far rise.

I got back in the saddle and rode across the smoky battlefield to join Jim Beckwourth and the major just as a trio of Texans were approaching through the chaparral the other way, under a parley flag.

I got there first. So you might say I saved West Texas more bloodshed that afternoon, because I'd already told Major Chivington what Colonel Slough had said about fighting Texas on his own when the men from Texas rode in with a proposal from Major Pyron.

Chivington read it, glanced up at the sky, and generously

announced, "My compliments to Major Pyron for the grand party he just threw for us, and I agree we don't have enough daylight left to make another dance worthwhile to either side. Tell him we agree to an overnight truce in order that both sides can care for their dead and wounded. But tell him that we propose to resume the fighting at first light, no matter whom we see out in front of us, understood?"

The officer in command of the delegation nodded and asked about the guns some of the boys might have left behind in their haste. Chivington laughed boyishly and replied, "Don't you worry, ah, Lieutenant. I'm sure we've a few men who can figure out how to load and fire even a fancy field gun all the way from France. Of course, if your Major Pyron would like to fight some more for them, in the daylight we have left . . ."

They didn't think Pyron wanted to. After they'd left, Chivington turned back to me, grinning like a kid who'd just swiped a basket of apples without getting caught, and said, "All right, we'd best get back to the Pigeon ranch and wait for Colonel Slough, Clark. I'll want you as a witness that I never captured one rebel gun *after* you told me Johnny Slough said the notion was just too big a boo for me to try."

I had to laugh, too. But I had to be fair. So I looked him straight in the eye and told him, "I saw what you just done, Major. Before we mean-mouth Colonel Slough, it's my considered opinion you were just now lucky as hell. I don't know how else to explain at least a battalion of grown men firing on one charging target and somehow *missing* it!"

Chivington shrugged and said, "The Lord is with me, son. Our cause is just and Jesus has greater plans for me than my dying in battle. Just you wait and see."

I did and, looking back, it's sort of a shame they *didn't* kill him down New Mexico way, whilst he was still the hero who'd saved Colorado for the Union.

He wasn't done yet, that first day, even though Major Pyron would later write: "Had it not been for that devil, Chivington, and his Pikes-Peakers, the gold fields would have been ours. . . ."

But long before anyone on either side would get to write such memoirs they'd have to live through the rest of the war.

It was tough to do so without looking like a sissy. When we got back to the Pigeon ranch with our dead, our wounded, and them swell mountain howitzers, we found Colonel Slough waiting for us there with seven hundred mounted troopers he'd forged on ahead with. I was expecting him to chew Major Chivington out just awful. But when he spied those captured guns and the extra horses and mules we'd rounded up, and noticed how few men Chivington had lost whilst accomplishing all this, he just laughed and called Chivington a ferocious lunatic the Good Lord must have taken quite a liking to.

As they dined on roast chicken supplied by the Pigeons, it was Jim Beckwourth who morosely pointed out, "One robin doesn't make it Spring for certain, gents. Whilst you've been slapping one another on the back I'd had me a word or more with the prisoners. Some Texas boys talk mighty cocky to a gentleman of color. But even allowing for some bragging, their Colonel Scurry left Santa Fe with as many men as we come over Raton Pass with and there's no way we kilt a quarter that number, so far. Come morning, that Pyron who's so concerned about his dead and wounded will have reinforcements. The Texicans are all mounted. So Pyron is likely to have us outnumbered, again."

Colonel Slough nodded and said, "I know. I don't want to make my stand here, lest I risk my prisoners and captured field guns as well as innocent civilians."

He turned back to Chivington and said, "My seven hundred and I ought to be able to hold until the rest of the Firsters catch up, given a halfway strong position. Meanwhile, Major, if you'd like to take your own battle-tested troops out to, ah, do whatever it is you do against the enemy's flanks or rear . . ."

Both officers grinned like mean little kids. Jim Beckwourth protested, "I'd never divide my command if I only commanded a tad over a thousand, all told, Colonel."

Slough said, "It's a good thing you're not in command, then, Jim. We know we're taking a chance. You don't win fights by playing it safe. Lock yourself in a cupboard and nobody will ever punch you in the nose. On the other hand, you won't punch *him* worth mention, either, and meanwhile he'll be free to loot your house.''

Stabbing the fuzzy map on the table in front of him, Slough said, ''Our mission is not to crawl into a cupboard. It's to keep those rebel sons of bitches this side of Raton Pass come hell or high water. To move through Raton Pass, Sibley must secure Fort Union. To get to Fort Union he has to get through us, and *this* bitty pass, here, what's its name?''

One of the Pigeons knew. The best wagon route from where we were to Fort Union ran through Glorieta Pass, an otherwise unimpressive notch through unspectacular but damned steep wooded ridges. Colonel Slough thanked the local *ranchero* and said, ''Very well, then. We'll form our lines in the chaparral to either side of the wagon trace leading on through Glorieta Pass. Between our six-shooters, seven hundred carbines, and those captured howitzers . . .''

Then one of the junior officers who'd charged with Chivington that afternoon cleared his throat for attention and, once he got it, said, ''We only got some of their field guns and hardly any of their ammunition, Colonel. Those Johnnies firing grape across the field at us used up all the powder they had with 'em before we ran them back from their guns. I suspect that's *how* we ran them back from their guns.''

Another officer said, morosely, ''In sum, we're talking about them coming at us close to two-to-one with any field guns they still have set to fire, and our captured ordnance vice versa.''

Slough sighed and said, ''Well, we've still got to try.''

That was when Major Chivington said, ''I know what we'd best do, then. Me and my boys had best circle around behind those dastardly rebels and just capture their ammunition train.''

Everyone laughed but Jim Beckwourth and me.

We knew the preaching militant and fighting fool meant exactly what he said. John Chivington had no sense of humor worth mention.

I failed to get much sleep that last night at the Pigeon ranch. As I lay in my bedroll under the stars, some Mex gal near a

distant camp fire kept strumming a Spanish guitar and wailing
about her pal, Oma. Seeing she wouldn't let me sleep, I carried
my six-guns and Sharps cavalry carbine over to the nearest
night fire to make sure they'd stand by me in the morning
should push come to shove.

It was a good thing I did. I hadn't fired a shot so far but
somehow I was missing three infernal caps.

The famed Sharps rifles and carbines were designed by
Christian Sharps, who'd learned his trade under the famous
John Hall of Cincinnati. The Hall breechloaders won the Mexican War. As it ended, Sharps came out with his own improved
design. His guns loaded so easy and shot so straight that to this
day they call an unusually fine shot a Sharps Shooter.

Until way more recent they just didn't make ammo rounds in
one neat piece. The powder, ball, and some wadding went into
a greased paper cartridge. When loading up, I tore open the
end away from the ball with my teeth, so's any handy flame
could get at the powder. In *real* olden times a flint lock supplied the sparks as set the charge off and blew the bullet out.
In the 1820s a Scotchman named Forsythe invented the handier
percussion cap. As refined by another Scot named Shaw, the
copper percussion cap had the flintlock beat by miles. It looked
sort of like a tiny top hat made for a bug to wear, save for the
fact that the top, not the bottom of the bitty top hat was open.
Inside, down where the hat brim and bottom of the cap went,
they put just a dab of mercury fulminate. The delicate detona-
tor was sealed with tinfoil and a drop of shellac. Caps were
kept dry but a gun was never capped before it was loaded if the
user valued his fingers and eyeballs worth mention. He could
even wind up with a ball in his brain.

I replaced the caps I'd lost riding about all day. So now my
six-guns were set to fire good as any modern Peacemakers.
Straighter, as a matter of fact. Those old Walker Colts had nice
long barrels with a fine balance. A Texas Ranger had helped
Sam Colt design that model.

My good old Sharps hadn't thrown her cap. I replaced the
old one anyway. It only fired single-shot but, thanks to its neat
design, it reloaded sudden as well as breech. The breech

opened vertical, sliding in a mortise cut in the steel receiver. The trigger guard acted as a lever. When you cranked it down the block was lowered to let you just shove the whole paper cartridge in the chamber. You didn't have to tear the paper open. As you raised the block back up, a knife edge built right into the Sharps cut the base off neat as any shears might have. Then all you had to do was thumb a cap on the nipple with the hammer set on safe, cock her all the way back when required, and pull the trigger. A Sharps Shooter could get off eight or ten rounds a minute with a little practice and, best of all, he didn't have to stand up and expose his position, like a cuss with a muzzle loader had to, every time he reloaded that long barrel with the long ramrod.

I recounted all the caps and cartridges I still had. I was hoping I'd never be called upon to fire that many rounds when old Four Eyes, the lance corporal who drew maps, came over to squat by me in the flickering firelight. He looked worried. He said, "I just had me a look at those old boys they got lashed to that captured gun limber."

I put my guns aside and got out some tobacco as I observed, "That's not the best move you could have made, just before your bedtime on the eve of another battle, Four Eyes. Some of them old boys we lost this afternoon looked depressing enough, fresh kilt."

Four Eyes said, "I noticed. They tell me you were with Ben Jung when he died from that busted spine."

I started to ask who Ben Jung was. Then I nodded and said, "Right, the kid who worked in the drugstore in less trying times. I can't say for sure what he died from. Busted spine sounds sensible as anything else. What about him?"

Four Eyes stared soberly into the glowing coals as he softly told me, "I've never seen a man die. What's it like?"

I laughed incredulously and replied, "How in thunder would I know? It was that drugstore clerk as died this afternoon, not *me*. I can't even say for certain *when* he died, let alone what it felt like. One minute he was talking to me and then I noticed he wasn't. There was a dying Texican nearby who didn't have much to tell me about the Great Beyond as he entered it, either.

I'm not sure either of 'em knew for certain they were dying. I know *I* couldn't tell, afore they *did*."

Four Eyes repressed a shudder and asked if I really thought there might be a Great Beyond. I said, "There *might* be folk living on the moon, like that professor says. If you're asking what I know for *certain* about dying, all I can tell you is that I mean to avoid it long as possible."

Four Eyes almost sobbed, "But sooner or later ain't we all fixing to be dead, Ross?"

I grimaced and said, "You sure are swell company late at night when a man's having enough trouble trying not to ponder unpleasant on the coming dawn. Look on the bright side, Four Eyes: if they kill you tomorrow you'll never have to lose any sleep over dying some *other* time, see?"

He said, pouty as a little kid who didn't want to go to bed, "I don't want to die, ever. It ain't fair of the Lord to create us so fragile that we don't even last a hundred years without busting!"

I said, "Think how pissed you'd feel if we only lived long as cats and dogs. It's the *thinking* about dying that makes us fear death, Four Eyes. Whether they're playing harps or feeling nothing at all, them old boys lashed to that gun limber ain't half as scared of death as *we* are right now."

He brightened and asked, "Do you admit you're at least a mite afraid of what's coming, Ross?"

To which I could only reply, "I'm scared skinny. I know that even if I live through tomorrow I still got to die *some* damned day. But you don't see me crying, because I figured some time back that crying won't do you half as good as fighting the good fight one day at a time."

"Then you've made your peace with Death?" he asked, wistful-eyed.

I laughed, a mite bittersome, and went on tamping my pipe as I told him, "I've made up my mind not to die, as long as I'm alive. That way I don't have to dwell on dying afore it happens and since I likely won't know I'm dead, once I am, I don't ever expect to enjoy any personal experience with Death."

I handed him the tobacco pouch and told him to put that in his pipe and smoke it. He told me I was no more help than those dead boys over on that gun limber and got up to wander off and pester someone else. I went back to my bedroll and tried not to think about death some more. I'd just fallen asleep, it seemed, when Jim Beckwourth woke me up at first light to go out and get shot at some more.

Chivington's four hundred, what was left of 'em, had ridden well clear of the Pigeon ranch by the time the sun was all the way over the jaggedy rim off to our east. Jim and me were even further out, on point, along with a *vaquero* called Hernando who hated Texicans and knew the country way better.

We were still playing blindman's buff with Scurry's spread-out guerrillas. Major Chivington's plan was to work our way clean around 'em without letting them know we'd hived off from Slough's main column. Hernando held this was way easier said than done.

Having hunted many a stray up many a canyon in these parts, the wiry young Mex knew a man on horseback could work his way most any damned where if he really had a mind to. There was an embarrassment of routes to choose, from well-blazed wagon traces to unmarked game trails calling for brush-popping.

Jim told Hernando, "Them Texicans should have patrols out ahead along most any trail a rabbit could negotiate, albeit only fanned out a mile or less along their main line of advance, and we know they're advancing towards Glorieta Pass, see?"

Hernando could. He wasn't stupid, even if he hadn't had any military drill in recent memory. Jim then instructed, "The rebel colonel's main body of riders will want to stick to fairly well-marked trails, if only to keep from getting scattered. Scurry's weak link ought to be them guns and supply wagons he's got to be hauling along with him. Do you follow my drift, Hernando?"

The *vaquero* nodded but said, "*Si, pero* is more than one good way for to haul wagons through these hills, *amigo negro.*"

Jim Beckwourth didn't get sore. He knew the kid had called him his black pal, in Spanish. He said, "Them Texicans can't know this country as well as you, Hernando. Forget sneaky trails and study on any you'd sort of follow *natural*, coming up out of Santa Fe with Fort Union and Raton Pass in mind."

Hernando did and decided, "I got two wagon traces they could be on. Which one do you wish for to scout, *amigo negro*?"

Beckwourth swore, laughed, and said, "Let's go for the most direct route and let's do so pronto."

So Hernando led us on through the high chaparral a ways, then he swung off into even rougher country. Jim directed me to hang back and steer Chivington the right way. So I did. I'd just got my pipe lit when I spied the red-and-white guidon coming across the chaparral at me. As the major loped forward to ask me what was up, I pointed at the fluttersome banner with my pipe stem and explained, "That Mex knows the way through some canyon. Do we really have to ride on with our colors showing, Major? I mean, we know who we are, and don't you reckon we ought to let the other side guess?"

Chivington frowned thoughtfully at me, a frightening experience, and then he smiled in a surprisingly boyish way and told me I was right. He turned in his saddle to order his battalion guidon furled and cased. Then he told me to lead on. So I did. Neither Jim nor that *vaquero* were trying to cover their sign, so it was easy enough to trail them. It's a good thing it was. Major Chivington kept prodding me to bust after them faster.

When we finally caught up with Jim and Hernando they weren't in any canyon. They'd dismounted on what seemed a flat stretch of fairly tall nut pine and juniper. As they saw us coming Jim signaled us to dismount and come in on foot. Major Chivington and me strode forward at the head of the dismounted column. It still made for a real tingle when we suddenly wound up staring down a thousand feet. The slick young Mex had led us around by way of the mesa tops to approach the deep canyon and the wagon trace running along its bottom from the side. The sides rose a good thousand feet, or a hundred flights of steps, if anyone had seen fit to build a stairway up to us from that skinny double thread of dust down yonder. The canyon walls weren't sheer, on second glance. The canyon had cut through shale and even softer clay, so its walls sloped at about the same angle as the roof of two hellishly big barns built by gods, close together, with just that narrow roadway way down yonder to separate 'em.

There wasn't a sign of movement in the dusty depths. Chivington fretted till Jim Beckwourth soothed, "Nobody's been along that wagon trace since dawn, Major. Look how the night dew's crust is still even as a fresh coat of tan paint over all them ruts."

Chivington brightened and said, "By George, we got here *first*—assuming they're not pushing up some *other* confounded canyon, that is!"

Beckwourth asked Hernando about that. The young Mex admitted he knew of yet another canyon, off on the far side of this mesa we were on top of. When he added that the other one would take them way out of their way Beckwourth sighed and said, "We'd best make certain. I never underestimate the stupidity of any man who thinks the Lord created me to serve him mint juleps and grin like I enjoyed it."

He turned to me. "Ross, you'd best scout down along *this* rim whilst Hernando and me scout that other canyon. No matter which way they're coming they ought to move their own scouts out on flank, which'd mean up here, see?"

I said I did. As Jim and the Mex rode off I told Major Chivington I'd be back sudden if I spied anyone coming up the canyon. He allowed that was jake with him and called his officers in for a powwow as I knocked my pipe out on a boot heel, remounted my cordovan, and rode south along the canyon rim.

I hadn't gone far when I heard a distant rumble and, now that I was getting used to wars, I never looked up at the cloudless sky for further instruction. I judged most of the noise was coming from the general direction of the Pigeon ranch. I knew Colonel Slough had moved out from there by this time.

I'd got a couple of furlongs away from the outfit hunkered along the rim back yonder when I spied a flash of movement amongst the nut pines ahead. I reined in, dismounted, tethered

my pony to a handy juniper, and eased forward, my Sharps at
port arms and a Colt riding either hip. When I heard someone
singing "Ole Black Joe," off-key, I got a bushy nut pine
between us and cocked my Sharps as he rode ever closer,
crooning:

> I's comin',
>     I's comin',
>         Do mah haid am bendin' low,
>             I hears their gentle voices callin',
>                 Ole . . . Black . . . Joe!

I saw what Jim Beckwourth had meant about mint juleps.
Being as white, myself, I understood a heap of white folk,
North and South, really did feel they were doing darkies a
favor by teaching them to fetch and carry so faithful when they
might have been under some fool banana tree along the Gold
Coast, just enjoying themselves.

As the singing Southron rode into view through the ever-
green branches I saw he was a good-natured-looking cuss in his
late twenties or early thirties, smooth-shaven but dusty-faced,
dressed halfway between a soldier and a cowhand. Like myself, he wore a uniform blouse over his cowherding duds, only
his was gray with black buttons. He was doubtless dressed that
way for the same reasons Jim and me were expected to look
sort of military, coming back in.

I didn't want him going back in. So I stepped out from
behind my tree to call out, "Howdy! I'd rather capture you
than shoot you. So have the courtesy to grab some sky with
your gun hand, Tex."

He should have. But he went for his saddle gun instead. So
when I fired he went one way and his pony lit out another. I
leaned the spent carbine in the fork of a juniper and drew a
six-gun to move in for a closer look at what I'd just wrought.
As I got about point-blank range he suddenly rose to his feet,
hatless and even dustier, to spit and observe, "Do Jesus, they
make bitter dust in these parts. Tastes like spiderwebs smell,
don't it?"

I said, "Sure does. Did I hit you, just now?"

He smiled crookedly at me and replied, "Sure did. Can't say just where. I feel as awful all over. I ain't sure I want to be captured, Yankee."

I shrugged and said, "Well, you are, just the same, and I wish you wouldn't call me a Yankee. I started out in Tennessee, and how I wound up in this outfit is too long and tedious to go into. I'm fixing to take you back to my battalion now."

He said, pleasantly enough, "No you ain't," and that was when I saw the pepperbox pistol he was holding in his left hand, down along his side. I'd assumed a man gripping his middle with his right hand meant no harm. As the southpaw Southron swung his pepperbox up I fired again. He reeled but stayed on his feet long enough to stare glassy-eyed and mutter, "Aw, shit, *now* look what you've gone and done!"

Then he was down again and, this time, he wasn't about to get up. I made certain of that. Then I looked about for the paint pony he'd been riding. To this day I can't tell you where it ran off to. But I doubt it could have run back to his outfit. For when I scouted closer to the canyon rim I spied his outfit coming up the wagon trace far below, like a long train of ants on their way to a sugar bowl.

I mean, that Confederate supply column was *considerable*. Eighty-odd covered wagons and, counting the mounts of the outriders as well as stock hitched to those wagons, over five hundred horses and mules, all moving at a mile-eating trot on the sound of distant guns!

I ran to my own mount and got back to Major Chivington even faster. He ordered everyone with us to mount up, but quietly, with no bugle calls to alert the oncoming rebel column.

I figured he meant for us to ride back along the rim to where the canyon road wound up out of the depths. I said so when I noticed we weren't going anywhere in particular. Chivington drew his sword, pointed out across all the wide-open nothingness, and said, "We'll let the slavocrats get abreast of us and then we'll hit them with a flank attack, charging downhill, see?"

I wasn't the only one there who gasped in horror. One of the captains protested, "You can't be serious, Major! That's no *hill*, it's an almost sheer *cliff*!"

Chivington said, "Piffle. Can't be steeper than forty-five degrees, and if a few of us lose our footing, we all want to get to the bottom anyway, don't we?"

The captain said there was no power on earth that was going to make him ride over the edge aboard a pony without one pair of wings to call its own. Then a rider further south called out, "I see them! Clark was right and, kee-rist will you look at the *size* of that wagon train!"

Chivington did. Then he reined back from the edge and called out, "Column of files and follow me!" as he rode along the rim to string his battalion out in an even longer line than all those riders and wagons made along the road below us. I was riding a couple of men behind the major when he suddenly swung back to the rim, saw we were in as flanking a position as we'd ever manage, and simply called out, "Charrrrrge!" as he followed the tip of his flashing sword over the edge to drop out of sight in a cloud of dust.

I heard myself sobbing, "Oh, shit!" as I spurred my own pony. For one Christ-awful moment, as I stood in the stirrups staring down into that dreadful abyss, I was sure I'd just killed the both of us!

But as the wild rider who led us must have known, or hoped, most ponies can in fact get down a forty-five-degree slope good as oversized kids on playground slides. I say *most* because a few of the boys did spill and what Chivington had said about us all winding up at the bottom, either way, sure applied. None of the riders who spilled were actually killed, and only a few of the ponies who'd rolled had to be shot, in the end. Most of us made it all the way down with our mounts hunkered on their rumps as they plowed a bodacious amount of dust with their stiff forelegs.

We must have struck the Texicans along the wagon trace as a mighty ominous wave, for most of 'em ran up the far slope, yelling like gals who'd just had mice run under their skirts. Those who stood their ground never had a chance, as they went down in lonesome little Alamos in the wave of slashing Army Blue.

I shot one poor cuss on the far slope before I realized what he meant with both hands up like that. Then, before I even had my breath back, it was all over.

Major Chivington called me over where he sat his lathered mount near an overturned wagon and a knot of hangdog prisoners. He yelled, "Clark, I want you to ride like the wind to Colonel Slough and the others! Tell him what we've just done. Then tell him I'll be on my way to join him as soon as we tidy up here. Any questions?"

I said, "Yessir. What do you mean by 'tidy up' and how long is it likely to take, in case the colonel asks?"

Chivington waved his sword grandly and explained, "We have to make certain none of this ever falls into rebel hands again. Tell Slough I make it sixty wagonloads of food and supplies, along with two dozen ammunition wagons. I mean to salvage some of the ammunition. What's left ought to help us get rid of the salt pork and hard tack once we set the wagons afire."

I stared soberly down the long line. Some of the disarmed rebels were helping our boys line things up again along the wagon trace. As if he'd read my mind, Chivington said, "All these prisoners are apt to slow us down beyond endurance. We only have five hundred horses and mules to bayonet, but . . ."

"You aim to *bayonet livestock*, sir?" I cut in.

He sheathed his sword with a shrug and replied, "I'm not about to expend five hundred rounds of *ammunition* when there's no need to. I expect Colonel Slough's a mite worried about us, son."

I grimaced, whirled my pony around, and lit out up the canyon lest I have to watch them bayonet all those horses and mules. I could only hope he meant to treat his human prisoners less severe.

As I rode on to the sound of distant guns the way led mostly higher, so the canyon walls to either side kept sinking lower until at last I found myself loping across more open range. It

was bumpy, with the rounded crests of the swells overgrown
with brushy nut pine that could hide a multitude of sins. The
draws were cluttered even worse with a tanglewood of willow,
cottonwood, and thorn. As I rode I read the ruts ahead of me
for any sign I'd been preceded. I didn't spy any till the wagon
trace I rode was joined at a sharp angle by a narrower trail
pounded deeper by both shod and cloven hooves. Many a hoof
print looked fresh, and when I spied flies hovering over still-
damp horse apples I knew I had to be close behind Texas riders
who'd followed a rougher, but likely more direct, route up
from Santa Fe.

That reminded me I was wearing a Union hat and blouse.
Being this seemed hardly the time or place for such formal
attire, I reined in off the trail and dismounted amid some scrub
to take of my blue blouse and roll it into the bedroll lashed
athwart my saddlebags. There wasn't much I could do about
the hat. But once I'd removed the crossed swords under the
Roman numeral and put the pin in my shirt pocket, the hat
didn't look like all that much.

I rode on, trying to read the rumbles on the wind, for I
wasn't out to ride through Scurry's Texans to get to Slough's
Firsters. But it's mortal hard to pick one's way across a battle
zone without anyone else noticing, even when you know what
you're doing.

I didn't. So a furlong on I rounded a bend to meet up with
a couple of old boys on foot. One was helping the other as they
both limped toward me. As I reined in, I saw both wore bloody
bandages as well as the civilian costumes of West Texas hands.
The one doing the helping had one arm in a sling. His pal was
hobbling along with one foot in a dusty boot and the other
wrapped in filthy rags. The one who looked less confused
called out to me, "Hey, reb, might you have a drop of water,
for Gawd's sake?"

I unlashed a full canteen and handed it down to the one with
a gimp leg and two arms that worked. He blessed me and my
kin back to Mother Eve and, to his credit, offered it to his pal,
who'd been walking all that way for the both of them. I let
them both swill some before I asked how far they'd come and

what might have happened to their ponies. The one with the wounded arm said, "Place calt Glory Something. Make it seven miles or more back up this durned old trail and I'll still say we've trudged further. Colonel Scurry ordered us to dismount and advance afoot, the stupid cuss. That's the last we seen of the pony. The Yanks up ahead can't be militia, like we was told. We got 'em outnumbered and outgunned and they still won't fall back, the stubborn sons of bitches!"

The one who looked like he'd stopped a round from a Sharps with his skin held the canteen up to me as he agreed, "They must be regulars from Fort Union. We been fighting 'em all morning on this big flat patch of waist-high chaparral, and here it is afternoon and just listen to them guns back yonder."

I told them to keep the canteen and asked where they thought they were headed in such condition. The one with the gimp leg said, "We should have met up with our rear echelon by this time. Say, might that be where you just come from, reb?"

I nodded and said, "The wagons are down this trace a piece. If I were you boys I'd fall out in some shade beside the trail and wait for someone to find you. Ain't nobody I know of within easy walking distance. And now I got to get it on up the road, so good luck and hasta your vista, as we say in Texas."

I rode on before they could correct me. I knew I couldn't count on my Tennessee twang passing me off for a Texan. Texas had been mostly settled by folk from the deeper south. Those west of the Brazos had only taken up cows after they'd noticed how poorly cotton grew in such dry country. Lest I bump noses with some officer or even a clear-headed corporal who knew the answers to questions I'd be stuck with, I cut away from the trail to see if I could circle wide and get to my own side without having to ride clean through the Confederacy.

I found I could. As I kept the rumble of gunfire on my left flank the already hilly range ahead got steeper. But I was able to pick our way around the thicker clumps of timber and bigger outcrops of rock until the slopes began to drop off ahead and I realized we'd made it atop a long, low ridge. I only had to circle a mite before, sure enough, we cut the game trail along the mountain ridge. Deer like to travel along ridges because they can dash off downhill no matter which way something hunting 'em approaches, *uphill*.

I swung my cordovan mare more or less north along the ridge. To tell the truth I was paying more attention to the distant sounds of battle than I was the afternoon sun. The sounds weren't all that distant, now.

As I ran the ridge I found myself wondering why I was behaving so determined about a war I hadn't finished deciding about. Nobody on either side had ever done me really dirty and the rebs I'd met so far had seemed neither better nor worse than your average Firster. I still rode on, not knowing what else I was supposed to do, as I cussed that stupid Bama Bob and the stupid fix he'd gotten me into with the kin of that dead Mex gal. For, left to my own devices, I'd have been fixing to get off work at that tannery about now. It had to be after five in the afternoon if the low sun over yonder meant anything.

Then I topped a knoll along the ridge and suddenly had a clearer view of the broad, flat valley we'd been skirting. I reined in for a long sober stare as I muttered, "Jesus H. Christ, ain't that something!"

For I could see better, from up here, than either opposing commander down yonder, what they thought they were doing. Thanks to the waist-high scrub, a heap of men were almost invisible until they gave away their position with a big cotton ball of gun smoke. There was quite a haze of such smoke hanging above the whole valley by now. But, as I said, the individual puffs showed me where gents were till I had the way the fight was going straighter in my mind. The flags helped, too. I knew the boys around the Stars and Stripes near the blue silk banner of the Firsters had to be Colonel Slough's stand. The Texans didn't fly the famous Stars and Bars; they must have figured the Lone Star flag of Texas was good enough to fight Yankees. I saw company guidons and platoon pennants fluttering as well. It all added up to an old-fashioned shoot-out betwixt opposing skirmish lines, with Scurry banking on his greater numbers to press an unimaginative but ferocious frontal assault. From up here I couldn't tell who was winning.

I rode on along the ridge till I was well behind the Union line and then I put my Union blouse back on, pinned the Firster badge to my hat, and tore downhill faster than I'd ever meant to before I noticed how steep it was.

I would later learn Scurry had attacked Slough's seven hundred in mid-morning, with over a thousand tough Texans. Neither side had as many left this late in the afternoon. The Firsters had slowly given ground, a dead Texan at a time. Neither side had shown a trace of cowardice or a lick of common sense, so far, as I bee-lined toward the blue silken banner I saw outlined against gunsmoke and, sure enough, caught up with Colonel Slough.

He was afoot, his charger having been shot out from under him some time before. I dismounted and tethered my own mount behind a screen of high chaparral before I joined Slough and his staff. A man down the line a piece yelled, "Oh, Mother!" and dropped from sight with both hands covering his face.

I told Slough what Major Chivington had just done.

Slough grinned wolfishly through the smoke-grime, making his face look blacker than Jim Beckwourth's and said, "Thank God! The last thing I'd want those sons of bitches to have would be *more* ammunition! They've been shooting lead like hail at us for hours with no sign of a letup! The only edge we have comes courtesy of Mr. Christian Sharps. A lot of them began this battle with stand-up muzzle-loaders. Never stand in waist-high cover with a Sharps carbine sighted on you within three hundred yards, son."

I said I wouldn't and added, "Major Chivington says he means to hang on to some of their ammunition and join us, here, as soon as he tidies up down yonder. That's what the major calls bayoneting livestock, tidying up."

Colonel Slough grimaced and said, "All right, he's a diamond in the rough. Soft-hearted sissies don't win fights, and the point is that he *won*."

Another Firster, disturbingly close, yelped like a kicked pup and flung his Sharps rooftop-high as he went down. Slough sighed and said, "Spine shot. We're going to have to pull back just a tad. The bastards have our positions pin-pointed again.''

He waved his bugler in and warned, ''Sound Retreat, but soft and not at all excited. Then count to exactly fifteen and signal Assembly.''

The bugler smiled wearily and said he knew what the colonel wanted. I wasn't as sharp about bugle calls then, but since I knew just what was going on I had no trouble moving my pony back to a safer position. You've heard 'em blow Retreat if you've ever been near an army post when they were lowering the flag in the evening. Assembly's the same call they use to line the boys up for roll call in the morning. After it sounded, that noisy afternoon, I couldn't see much difference. But on the other hand, down there on the flat, I couldn't see much of anything, and that was doubtless the colonel's reason. As the two sides swapped shots across the bushy tops of the chaparral, it took a spell for anyone to pick out a certain target. Once you knew exactly where an enemy was, you could nail him through the bush he was hunkered ahint. Chaparral can't stop bullets so well.

I found that out when some Texican bastard pinked my right thigh whilst I was hunkered ahint a considerable clump of juniper. I wasn't hurt bad at the time, and the sawbones told me later the juniper juice might have saved me from a mortified wound. Lots of the old boys wounded that day, on both sides, died weeks later, all fevered and pussed.

I didn't think it was fair of Texas to shoot me like so, since I hadn't been shooting at a soul since I blew away the teamster back in that canyon. Seeing they wanted to behave so ornery I got my own Sharps off my saddle and commenced to look for a likely target. It wasn't easy to spy one, though, betwixt all the gunsmoke, dust, and the way they stayed hunkered down in the spinach. I got my hat blown off standing taller for a better view. After I recovered my hat and studied the pinkie I could put through the hole in the crown, I'll allow I did some hunkering, myself.

The bugler moved everyone back again and as we reformed I found myself with old Four Eyes. He'd taken off his glasses and put 'em away under his blouse lest he lose 'em. So it took him longer than it might have to tell me, "I think you're wounded, Clark."

I said, "I noticed. Did you cut yourself shaving this morning?"

He touched the ugly scab along his left cheekbone and said, "It only hurt a mite as it was first starting to dry. I suspect it was as likely a thorn as a bullet. But don't you dare tell my gal once we get back to Denver."

I laughed and assured him I'd bear witness to the bodacious sword fight he'd had with General Sibley in the flesh. He said, "It's a funny thing, but, you remember that conversation we had back at the Pigeon ranch?"

I said, "I do, you depressing cuss."

He continued, "I know what you mean, now. I've seen at least a dozen boys die around me today and you were right. Each time it happened it scared *me* way worse than it could have scared *them*!"

I said I was scared enough and I didn't think this was any time to get cocky. Something buzzed by us like a big humming hornet and I said, "See what I mean?"

Four Eyes said, "I got that figured, too. If you can hear a bullet it ain't meant for you. You'll never hear *nothing* when they *kill* you. That's what being killed means, see?"

I said, "Hold on. Something's up," because I'd just spied Colonel Slough standing taller than usual a few yards off. Some of his staff help had broken cover, too. They sure looked vulnerable against the gold-and-lavender sky. The sky was fixing to set, but it wasn't too dark to shoot, yet.

I raised my own head higher. That was when I spied a trio of Texas riders coming through the chaparral toward us under a white parley flag. Four Eyes and me knew nobody would fire at us with their own delegation so exposed. So we stood all the way up and ambled over to see what Colonel Scurry wanted from Colonel Slough.

What he wanted was a cease-fire. The young Texican officer with a rooster-tail plume and crossed sabers pinned to his ten-gallon hat pointed out that night was coming, a heap of boys on both sides had already fallen, and asked if we'd like to call it a day.

Colonel Slough could barely keep from laughing out loud as he replied, "You're out of ammunition! My first battalion jumped your supply column hours ago and you rebels don't have a keg of powder or a bag of beans this side of Santa Fe! We were wondering why you'd stopped firing the field guns you had left."

The Texican smiled down sheepishly and replied, "You boys haven't lobbed any cannister shot at us in recent memory, neither. I'll allow you Yanks have stopped us, for now, if you'll allow we can still claw you good unless you'd like to see us back off gentle."

Slough asked them to spell it out plainer. The dapperly, dusty Texican said, "We withdraw with our dead, our wounded, and full honors. You leave us alone and we leave you alone, this side of Santa Fe. We can only speak for Colonel Scurry. Once we rejoin the main force under General Sibley, in Santa Fe . . . Well, nothing is certain in life, is it?"

Slough nodded soberly and said, "Let's try it this way. I'll give your commander till dawn before I advance on him again."

The Texicans all chuckled. Their spokesman said, "Begging the colonel's pardon, he wasn't *advancing* on *nobody* this afternoon. We were kicking the liver and lights outten you blue-bellies!"

Slough said, "That was when you had ammunition as well as more men still on their feet. I'm not an unreasonable man, reb. I'll tell you frankly it'll take me twelve hours or more to regroup in a manner more to my liking. So you may as well take advantage of the lull to do the same. But tell Scurry that come morning, hell or high water, I'll be moving on Santa Fe and anything between here and there with four hundred more riders and a heap of ammo Texas just delivered to *me*!"

This time none of them laughed. The dapper one saluted and said, "I'll pass your kind offer on to Colonel Scurry, sir. I don't think he's going to like it, though."

Slough shrugged and said, "We never took the field to make

*friends* with any of you glorified bandits. We were sent to kill
or capture every last one of you.''

As they rode off, one called back, defiantly, ''You'll have to
catch us first, Yankee!''

Colonel Slough reached for a smoke, murmuring, ''That can
be arranged, now that Sibley would seem to have shot his
wad.'' Then he suddenly laughed like a mean little kid and
added, ''By God, we've *done* it, boys! We've fought 'em to a
standstill and sent 'em south with their tails betwixt their legs!
Now that I've field guns to work with as well, I mean to free
Santa Fe and chase those sons of bitches all the way back to
their Alamo!''

He lit his cigar and chortled, ''Then I mean to take their
damned Alamo, too. That'll learn 'em to mess with Colorado!''


Like a heap of old boys who've grown used to winning,
Sibley's chastised Texicans proceeded to run like hell once
they'd been turned around by the Firsters. Scouting out ahead
of Chivington's advance battalion with Jim Beckwourth, I
spied more signs of hurried flight than resistance as we pushed
on to Santa Fe.

Sibley's rear guard was fixing to leave Santa Fe by way of
the back door as rode in the front. Most of the populace seemed
happy to see us. During his so-called military occupation of
Santa Fe, old Sibley had robbed every bank in town.

There was some scattered sniping our first few hours in
town. One sniper we rounded up was a ragged-ass Mex who
couldn't rightly say what *he'd* been doing up in the bell tower
with a rifle. We put him against the wall with the handful of
Texas irregulars who hadn't known when to quit. Whe I say *we*
I mean the outfit, of course. Jim Beckwourth and me were
south of town with some of the other scouts by the time those
particular prisoners were shot. We found most of the rebel
forces had known when to quit. They'd lit out down the Rio
Grande along with most everything that hadn't been nailed
down. So we secured the area five miles south of Santa Fe and
rode back for our well-earned supper.

What I most recall about Santa Fe, aside from all that confounded guitar music, is the cobwebby smell of dry 'dobe
blended with the nose-twanging scent of hot tamales cooked in
corn husks. They must cook something else down yonder now
and again, but all I remember is hot tamales. That and what
happened to Four Eyes.

I didn't see it. They told me about it that evening, as I was
sitting on some tile steps along the main plaza, eating a hot
tamale and sipping *cerveza*, which is what they call beer in
Santa Fe. Four Eyes had been picked off by a sniper, smack in
front of the Governor's Palace, a long low structure of mud
bricks and old sun-silvered logs. They had his body wrapped in
a tarp out back of the looted bank they were using as a clinic
now. They said they meant to bury him in the one Protestant
churchyard in town, come morning.

Mayhaps they did. I never attended. I'd never really gotten to
know the depressing cuss and he hardly needed me to tell him
what it might feel like to be dead, now. They'd said he'd been
hit in the back of the skull by a .52 buffalo round. I agreed there
was no way he could have felt a thing afore his brains and specs
had wound up on the front veranda of that Governor's Palace.

I'd have forgotten all about it had not the infernal chaplain's
assistant, a prissy lance corporal, tracked me down the next
morning to tell me the sky pilot wanted to talk to me about
Spencer. That was Four Eyes' given name, Cedric Spencer. I
was glad to see, once I'd followed the priss over to a tent
across the plaza, that they'd already planted Four Eyes. The
chaplain, a Methodist like Major Chivington but way milder-
looking, handed me a letter, saying, "We found this among
the late Cedric Spencer's effects. It appears to be the last letter
he wrote home to the girl he left behind. He was killed before
he ever got the chance to post it. Seeing you were his best
friend, Ross, and seeing there's no way to mail anything from
here in any case, I want you to hang on to this and see that the
poor boy's sweetheart gets it."

I started to say I'd never been that much of a friend to Four
Eyes. Then I decided *somebody* had to be, and put the torn-
open envelope away, under my blouse, as the chaplain droned

on. "I'm sure we can rely on you to break the news gently to the young lady, when the time comes. You might want to assure her his last thoughts were of her as he lay dying for the Union and Colorado."

I cocked an eyebrow and asked, "He was *thinking* of her, with his brains blowed out with his eyeballs?"

The chaplain sighed and said, "There are times a little white lie can be a great comfort, son."

I said, "I'll remember that the next time someone promises me a halo and harp of my very own, Captain. I got to see what they want me to do next about the enemy. I won't tell that gal in Denver about spattered brains. But I suspect I know what Four Eyes would have wanted me to say to her. So I'll do my best to comfort her, knowing nobody can, if the boy meant spit to her to begin with."

I found Jim Beckwourth inside the Governor's Palace instead of out front. Four Eyes had been picked off while they were setting up Colonel Slough's new headquarters there. Old Jim was sitting on a windowsill, smoking, whilst the colonel drew lines all over a big wall map for more important officers, like Chivington.

I asked the black senior scout what was up. Jim grimaced and said, "Poor Slough has a lot to learn. Sibley's headed down the Rio into the Jornada del Muerto country, provided and *only* provided he's dumb as hell. The Mexicans named that stretch of dry badlands down yonder a Journey of Death because that's the sort of country it is. Sibley will swing away from the Rio Grande this side of the Ladrons because he don't *want* to go to Old Mexico. He wants to get back to San Antone. He'll cut east up the Torrance Trail and follow the Fifteen-Mile Arroyo to the Macho, Pecos, and such into West Texas and *adios amigos Yanquis,* see?"

I said, "Ain't for me to see. Does the colonel know?"

Beckwourth nodded but said, "He thinks we can winkle the rebs into the desert badlands with their backs to Old Mexico if we keep up the pressure. He's sent for more ammo, supplies, and replacements. A lot *he* knows about the art of modern war."

I said Slough's simple plan made perfect sense to me. Beckwourth replied, "You're both talking old-fashioned war, where
the only consideration is winning. Didn't anybody tell you this
here Civil War is over *politics*, old son?"

I agreed most wars seemed to be, when one studied on it.
Jim saw I was still in the dark, thinking this world was run on
the level, and so he explained why Colonel John Slough of the
Colorado Firsters was never going to be allowed to follow up
on his stunning victories they would later lump together as the
"Gettysburg of the West" or the Battle of Glorieta Pass.

Colonel E.R.S. Canby, the West Point graduate Sibley beat
fair and square, had now been promoted to general to com-
pensate him for losing Santa Fe. The new commander ordered
us all back to Fort Union so's we could guard the approaches
to the Colorado gold fields from ferocious rebel raiders. That
let the rebel raiders we'd licked get clean away to Texas in case
they'd like to fight another day.

When Slough found out, after all the plans he'd made to
follow up on our victory, he was so ticked off he resigned his
commission and went home. Officers get to do that, the lucky
bastards.

Somebody still had to be in command of the regiment, even
as it limped back first to Fort Union and then home, Canby
having snatched a stalemate at best from the jaws of victory.
And that's how John Chivington came to lead us in the big
parade when we finally got back to Denver. By then the few
who remembered Colonel Slough at all considered him the
timid soul who'd tried to slow down the Hero of Glorieta Pass.

The parade was something, with the flags all fluttering, the
brass bands blaring, even ugly old maids blowing kisses at us
and little kids flinging posies, dirt clods, and horse turds—
albeit they mostly threw posies, after a few good licks from
their elders. Despite the way the regular army had low-rated
us, the *Rocky Mountain News* leaned over backwards to proclaim Glorieta Pass the greatest victory since Yorktown, if not
Marathon.

Whatever we'd done, we'd taken the wind out of General

Sibley's sails. In fairness to the fighting men of Texas, most of
'em fought and a heap of 'em died under the real General
Hood, further east. The Texas Brigade was shot up pretty bad
by Union General Thomas in the battle for Nashville, too.

Governor Evans expanded the Colorado Volunteers to two
fully active regiments, the First and the Third, with the Second
actually detailed to quartermaster, ordinance, and training du-
ties for now. The governor placed John Chivington in overall
command and wanted to make him a brigadier general. But the
War Department told Evans not to be silly. So Chivington
wound up a full colonel, which was high as militia ranks went
in those days. The three regimental commanders under him
only got to be lieutenant colonels. That allowed all the regular
army men commanding regiments a chance to look down on
'em from one pay-grade higher.

I kept up with such events by jawing with Jim Beckwourth
on the occasions we still met up in the Jayhawker. I'd been out
in the field with the Firsters longer than the six weeks I'd
signed up for. Being there was nothing to scout for once we got
back, they had to let me get back to more serious matters.
More serious to *me* at any rate.

I kept thinking about that unfortunate Mex gal who caught
one of Bama Bob's stray rounds with her trim figure. But when
I asked around town I found her kin had never come looking
for me at all. Knowing Bama Bob had manslaughtered their
kinswoman, a quartet of mighty morose Mexicans had caught
up with Bama Bob's best amigo, that coyote-face called Steinmuller, down by the stockyards. The copper badge who told
me about it said the results looked as if Steinmuller had been
captured by Cheyenne and turned over to the squaws.

The whole Mexican clan had left town directly after the
slaughter of Steinmuller. So that only left me one gal in Denver
I had to think about.

I'd naturally read the mushy letter Four Eyes had written to
her. After all, it was already opened and had no address on the
outside as yet. Once I had read it, I saw why the chaplain had
stuck me with the chore of delivering it. Methodist ministers
ain't supposed to let on they know about such matters, and old

Four Eyes sure wrote hot stuff for such a prissy-looking young gent.

His true love's name was Martha Nelson and she worked or lived above a notions shop near Larimer and 15th, a little over a city block from Cherry Creek. I found out that much the first night we were back in town. But I wanted to get my own affairs in order and take a real tub bath and neaten up a mite before I came calling with such dolorous news to relate.

They'd held my job for me at the tannery, and whilst my room at the boardinghouse had been let to another, the landlady had hung on to my things. We worked out an even cheaper deal for me, where I would stay up under her mansard roof with a bitty round window I could gaze from while standing on the bed.

It seemed sort of dumb to show up on a young gal's doorstep with flowers when you'd come with bad news instead of courting. On the other hand I'd been raised to never show up on any lady's doorstep without nothing. So as I left the barbershop fresh-trimmed and stinking of bay rum I picked up a bitty nosegay of violets at a corner stand and strode on over, just after suppertime, so's I'd not force anyone to invite me to set down to table with 'em or, contrarywise, keep anyone up past bedtime on a weeknight.

When I first got there I feared I'd made a really dumb move. For the notions shop facing Larimer was closed. A bitty sign in the window said they wouldn't be open again until seven in the morning. Ladies never shopped for needles, threads, and such before they'd finished their own morning chores, I reckon.

Then, as I stood there in the gloaming, cussing myself for a fool, I saw someone light a lamp behind the lace curtains upstairs. I explored around to one side and I found that, sure enough, a flight of steps led up the outside wall to living quarters above the shop. So I went on up and knocked.

When Martha Nelson opened that door, with the sunset shining in and the lamplight outlining her soft brown hair from behind, I knew at first glance why Four Eyes had fallen in love with her. It took me perhaps a few seconds longer. She stared soberly at the wilted envelope and soft of wilted flowers I was holding. Then her wide-set eyes of cornflower blue swept up the brass buttons of the military blouse I'd put on for the occasion and she murmured, "Oh, you'd be one of poor Cedric's comrades. Do come in, sir."

That's when I was *sure* I was in love with her. I'd never before met a gal so pretty, so smart, and so calm about it, all at once. She took both the flowers and love letter with a nod of thanks, and as I followed her into their parlor she introduced me to her sweet old mother and explained, "We have a visitor from Cedric Spencer's regiment, Mother, and look at these lovely violets they sent us!"

The old lady hopped up and out of the room like a little brown sparrow bird, twittering about coffee and cake.

By the time she got back with a swamping tray of refreshments, Martha had found out my name and seated me on a horsehair sofa next to her. She'd put the violets in a water jar with the blue chickory that had been there earlier. Violets and chickory look nice together. She hadn't taken the mushy letter out of its envelope as yet. I was hoping she might not, whilst I was still there. Four Eyes hadn't written any downright dirty words, but I couldn't see promising a gal you'd crush her to your breast until you became as one unless you'd gotten to know her mighty well, as they put such goings-on in the Good Book.

Her mother hauled another chair over and cut the cake for us on a bitty rosewood table between our knees and her own. As she did so, she prattled on about her being a widow and the two of 'em having come out to Denver from Maryland to avoid the war and open the shop downstairs. Without considering my words I frowned and asked Martha how long she might have known Four Eyes—I mean Cedric—if they'd only been out here such a short time.

She looked as if butter wouldn't melt in her mouth as she told me they'd bought this place from the builders Spencer had worked for as an architectural draftsman and salesman, when he wasn't playing soldier with the Firsters. She allowed she'd let him take her to a few church socials and, one time, to a regimental ball as his belle of the evening. She didn't sound as if he'd crushed her to him all that often.

I still owed it to the poor cuss to make him out the hero all dead soldiers deserve to be recorded as. As I et marble cake and sipped sugared cream with a dab of coffee in it, I told 'em how the brave young cuss had gone on fighting, after getting wounded, in the Battle of Glorieta Pass. I told them, truthfully enough when you studied on it, that most of the wounded had been sent back to Fort Union as we'd advanced on Santa Fe, making Four Eyes even more unselfish as he drew the very plans Colonel Slough had wanted us to follow in the liberation of the town. I didn't think they'd like to hear about scattered brains and eyeballs whilst they were eating, so I just said a sniper had shot him from a rooftop across the plaza. The old lady looked like she was fixing to bust out crying. She murmured, "Such a nice young man, with such a grand career ahead of him, too. It seems such a waste."

Martha said, softly, with just a little edge to her voice, "He had the makings of a novelist, too. I assume you've read this, Mr. Clark?"

That was when I saw she'd been reading the dead boy's last letter to her whilst I'd been droning on about how great he'd been. I started to deny it. As our eyes met I knew I'd just never be able to lie to Martha Nelson, no matter what she asked me. So I went on looking her smack in the eye as I replied, "Yes, ma'am. I know it was uncalled for. I only meant to seek out your name and address, but you know how hard it is to stop reading something, even when it ain't interesting."

She laughed, reminding me of robins singing in a rose bush, and said, "I'd have read it all the way through, too. As a matter of fact I just did. Would you believe me if I told you Cedric seems to have imagined I was fonder of him than he had any right to imagine?"

I nodded soberly but said, "His intentions were honorable and, seeing he had nobody else, what harm was anyone done, in the end?"

Her mother asked what we were talking about. Martha kept looking at me, as if for approval, as she quietly told the old lady the dead boy had asked her to be his true love. Her mother said, "Oh, dear. You weren't leading that poor boy on, were you?"

Martha protested, "Mother! How can you suggest such a thing?" I found myself explaining, "He never let on to me about anything at all improper, Mrs. Nelson. I reckon it was just the lonesome nights out in the field, with nothing to think about but getting back to Denver and, let's face it, the best-looking damsel he could have known."

The old lady laughed. Martha looked away, her cheeks suddenly rosier. I finished the last of the cup she'd poured me and added, "I got to get to work, too, come morning. So seeing I seem to have done all I come for, I'd best get it on down the road."

Nobody begging me to stay, I stood up and reached for my hat. The old lady stayed put. Martha rose to walk me to the door. When we got there she stepped out on the landing with me. The sky was royal purple and the stars were coming out now. Martha took one of my hands in both of hers and softly said, "Thank you for coming, Ross. I know how awkward this must have been for you."

I said it had only started out awkward and added, "I'd like to come back some time on an errand of my own, Miss Martha."

She asked what I meant, as if she didn't know. So I told her, "I got a good job here in town and I doubt I'll ever be called away to scout for the militia again. The war ought to be over any day now, and even if it ain't there's hardly anyone worth fighting on our side of the Mississippi. I know I may seem a tad young to you but I'm my own man, with nobody to answer to, and next election I'll be a voting man as well."

She went on holding my hand as she murmured, "That makes you just right for a seventeen-year-old silly like me, doesn't it? Are you saying you mean to come courting, Ross Clark?"

I said, "Unless you tell me not to, Miss Martha."

She said it was all right with her, as long as I kept it in mind that she wasn't at all like the gal in that fool letter. So I said I would, and that's how I got mixed up with less military notions.

The war was the last thing we were thinking about the first time I took her to church that Sunday. I'd meant what I'd said about having had enough of such bull.

*      *      *

The War Between the States was rougher on the eastern states than it ever was in the West. Prices went through the roof, and the West was where both money and a heap of things to buy with money grew. The Union paid for the war with western gold and silver, and even copper for its pennies, percussion caps, and telegraph wires. As if the hard-rock mines of the Front Range weren't enough to fuel the boom, they struck a rich coal deposit and some modest oil seeps down the other side of Pikes Peak. There seemed to be a bottomless market for the hides, tallow, and jerked beef of Colorado, too. I got another raise at the tannery. I needed it. Potatoes were selling for two bits a pound and nobody seemed to care. Prosperous Denver folk were willing to pay three dollars a gallon for strong spirits and had oysters shipped on ice from the main ocean at sixteen bucks a gallon!

After some financial flimflam on the part of the honest but not too sensible military government, Governor Evans, a well-to-do doctor from Illinois before Abe Lincoln appointed him, gave Colorado the needed stability to really get going. Most of us went on voting for Doc Evans long after the war and statehood. That's how come so many mountains, streams, streets, schools, and other good things in Colorado wound up named in his honor. He appointed honest judges and, like I said, made John Chivington head of the beefed-up territorial militia. If that was a mistake, so be it. The preaching militant wasn't ready to mess up, yet. All through the fall and winter after Glorieta Pass things just kept getting better and better.

More color was struck in the Colorado mountains. As placers and veins bottomed out in one place prospectors lucked on to gold in as many others. Silver was only selling at a sixteenth the price of gold, so nobody bothered with it. They panned the real stuff in California Gulch, Buckskin Joe, Strayhorse, Quartzville, South Fork, and dug it from mines called Pasteboard Greencloth, Maude Cyprian, Madame Featherlegs, Red Stockings, or John Barleycorn and, sooner or later, most all that gold passed through Denver.

Wages in the gold fields rose to six dollars a day. Gents paid

for drinks and more sinsome pleasures with raw gold dust, a
pinch betwixt thumb and forefinger being considered two bits'
worth, till Turner & Bobs opened their bank and Clark, Gruber
& Company were authorized to strike gold pieces with the
image of Pikes Peak on one face and the company seal on the
other. Nobody thought much of paper money in those days.

I wasn't even distantly related to the Clark who got to coin
his own money. So even with my raise at the tannery, I was
hard pressed to court Martha generous.

Courting tight or sportsome, I'd still gotten a better notion
what she and her mother were doing downstairs during business hours. They hadn't had enough of a grubstake to stock
anything grander than stuff that sold for less'n a dollar, even at
wartime prices. Meanwhile I'd been fooling around with scrap
leather, after work. Martha's mother wouldn't let me come by
more than thrice a week on work nights. I think I've made
mention of that winter I spent with a Mormon leather-worker
over in Utah Territory. In any case it naturally occurred to me
to make myself a new billfold when my old one got sort of
shabby. I made a few more things, just funning. I'd noticed
down in Santa Fe how Mexicans tooled leather belts. So I
chose some nice thick back-hide, overdone a mite in the tanning vats, and discovered that there wasn't all that much to
tooling twisty vines and curly spinach into thick leather, with
a good firm crust to it. I refit my old metal buckle to the result,
and the boys at the Jayhawker admired it so much I got orders
for more such belts, even when I figured the worth of my labor
at six bits an hour, or as much as a good mining hand might
make!

I couldn't sell stuff in saloons as fast as I could make it, of
course. So I brought some wallets, belts, and a change purse
I'd made special for Martha's mother to their shop, asking if
they wanted to see if they could sell it and we'd split the price.

Martha's mother kissed me on the cheek and said we had a
deal, even if I couldn't marry up with Martha before she was
eighteen and I was twenty-one, for land's sakes.

Thus it came to pass that by Christmas time I was in fair
financial shape and kissing Martha goodnight regular on that

back landing. I'd about forgot the war back east. The militia didn't even drill outside anymore, once it got to snowing serious that winter. Colorado winters are mighty cold, but otherwise not so bad. It's the *springtime* you got to watch, anywheres near the Rockies.

From time to time it could really rain out our way, and when it did, the combined waters of both streams made one big lake out of all the low ground between what's now called Capitol Hill and Little Palestine on the far side of the South Platte. Both so-called "heights" are just the natural level of the surrounding prairie where it was never carved deeper by flash flooding. So at the time of which I speak all the Denver there was was down on the flats of the natural flood plain. Most of downtown Denver still is. After what happened in the spring of '63 they dredged the bed of Cherry Creek way deeper. Some way the great flood we had in May would have done even more damage if we hadn't had that awful fire first, in April.

Denver had been layed out sensible enough, with wide streets running east and west, numbered, or north and south with names, such as Wazee, Blake, Market, Larimer, and so on. The thing that made the town such a tinderbox was the combination of balloon-frame construction with cedar-shingled roofing and the dry climate of the High Plains.

It's been generally agreed the first flames broke out in the Cherokee House, a hotel, on the night of April 19. Sparks soared high and drifted wide to come down on rooftops as easy to light as sun-and-wind-dried cedar usually is. So in no time at all we were having us one hell of a blaze. The "Great Fire Of '63" cut at least seventy buildings out of the heart of the city. It would have been way worse, we might have lost the whole fool town, if it hadn't been for Colonel Chivington and the Colorado Volunteers.

I was home in bed, asleep, when all hell seemed to be busting loose outside. I stood up to peer out my bitty round window, noticed the whole world seemed to be on fire, and got dressed sudden to go out and do something about.

Most every able-bodied man in Denver seemed to have had

the same grand notion. Bucket brigades were formed. I was near the warmer end of one, so I can tell you throwing a pail of water against the wall of a four-story frame on fire feels as futile as spitting into a blast furnace. The Volunteer Fire Department, such as we had, played its few fire hoses on the advancing flames with about the same results a dog might have managed, cocking its leg at a volcano.

Later, the *News* would make a lot out of our pioneer spirit and determination. I suspect we just went on fighting in vain because we didn't know what else to do.

Then all of a sudden the streets filled up with blue uniforms and Colonel Chivington seemed to be everywhere at once, riding his big thoroughbred at full gallop across the wet cobbles as he shouted orders and encouragement.

No further attempt was made to wet down roaring flames. Horses and mules were dragooned into service, and hitched to supporting beams to collapse buildings in the path of the flames like houses of cards. Kegs of powder meant to fight battles were used to blow other buildings flat. Chivington roared at men just standing around to pitch in and haul the infernal wreckage back from the inferno. So we did, and it worked. By dawn a heap of Denver's most substantial buildings had been reduced to smoldering rubble, and the loss of goods and services was going to shoot prices ever higher. But the rest of the city, along with all its wealth, had been saved, to send the stock of the militia and Colonel Chivington even higher.

They scored again that May when, just as things were getting back to normal after the fire, we caught some unusual weather.

The South Platte, springing as it did from snow-melt off the east face of the Front Range, always ran deep and swift in springtime. Folk allowed for that. One corner of the tannery yard stood under a few inches of muddy water, but that went with using the river as a handy drain for all them vats and, as a matter of fact, the spring of '63 had been dry, so far, for that neck of the woods.

That spring Denver was only about four years old, and nobody had considered what Cherry Creek might look like if it filled the wash and ran through all the way to the top. Nobody had ever seen it try, halfways. You could usually cross the braided stream dry-shod by judicious leaps from sandbar to sandbar. The prairie choke cherries it had been named for were already bittersweet memories, even then. Folk had built homes right up to the water's edge, assuming they knew where that might be.

We got a whiff of rain the day before the flood. Just enough to lay the dust and die away with a pretty evening rainbow to assure us all was well.

It had been raining like hell, for days, farther south. It was a Thursday evening, as I recall. I'd taken Martha to the Apollo Hall, Denver's first regular theater, above a saloon as catered to baser tastes. Tickets cost a dollar apiece and, afterwards, I took her to a German beer garden that wasn't fixing to be there twenty-four hours later. Martha wouldn't drink beer, but they served her cider and she joined in the singing, even though neither of us understood the words. To sing in a German beer garden you just have to know the tune and go "*ja, ja,*" some.

I got her home late, albeit it couldn't have been midnight yet. We tiptoed up the steps lest we wake her old mother, and I kissed her harder than usual till she giggled and told me to save *something* for after we could get hitched. So I let her go and headed back to my boarding house. But I never got there.

Nobody ever measured it, since it swept through Denver in the dark of midnight, but as best anyone could figure the wall of muddy water and churning debris must have topped twenty feet. The usual bed of Cherry Creek was four or five feet below street level in them days. So the next thing I knew I was swimming, or mayhaps flying. I just kept clawing and cussing as I went ass-over-tea-kettle in cold, wet, pitch-black panic until I found myself tangled up in tree branches, grabbed hold with such feeble strength as I still had, and started climbing until my head, at least, was above water.

I was one of the lucky ones. The city hall was washed away, with all its records. The city jail was ripped out by the roots along with the unfortunate prisoners in its drunk tank. Half the bodies were never found. Some wound up miles downstream.

The Methodist Church where Colonel Chivington served as
an elder and occasional preacher was smashed to kindling and
swept away. The law offices of Charles & Hunt bobbed off,
along with a junior partner named Haynes who'd apparently
decided to spend the night up there on a sofa. I say apparently
because they found his body buck-naked, halfway to Julesburg. They never found *her* body, if there'd been one to find.

The *Rocky Mountain News* was swept away, swirling and
whirling, with the flag on its roof still flying as if from a ship
at sea. Four newspaper men inside floated with it until they
finally escaped through a roof hatch, way downstream, to be
hauled ashore by cowhands who knew how to rope pretty
good. The incident resulted in a hell of a news story once they
were in shape to publish the washed-out paper again.

Some of the worst damage was done by the Larimer Street
bridge, torn from its foundations within yards of Martha's
place to go tearing through downtown Denver like a bodacious
blackboard eraser, rubbing out everything in its swirling path.

But neither Martha nor her widowed mother were drowned.
I only *thought* they were, as I climbed down out of that cottonwood into waist-deep but subsiding water to go flounder
back to their notions shop, cussing the darkness blinding me,
the water clawing at me, and, I have to admit, any Lord who'd
let such scary things happen!

That simple frame structure Four Eyes may well have designed had held like the Rock of Gibraltar, as most everything
else on the same block had gone bobbing off. All the muddy
water had churned high enough to wet the rugs upstairs and had
sure played hell with their poor little notions shop at street level.

It was too dark to notice such pettifogging details as I waded
up 15th Street, bawling for Martha like a lost calf. She heard
me long afore I got to the foot of them steps and ran down 'em
at me in just her nightgown, barefoot. When we crashed into
one another at last it felt so good to be young and alive in each
other's arms that we'd have likely wound up Biblical if there'd
been any place to lie down together in all that shin-deep slime.

We did it upstairs on the sofa, later, after we'd put her poor
weeping mother back to bed. Mrs. Nelson had noticed what the

flash flood had done downstairs and kept bawling that they
were wiped out. I told her she was talking dumb, since anyone
could see the three of us had come through alive with a roof
still over our fool heads, which was more than a lot of Denver
folk could say right now. It still took two hot toddies, made
with bourbon instead of rum, to calm her down enough so's
Martha and me could make love out front in the soggy dark.

After we had, Martha cried, of course, and said she'd never
be able to look me in the eye again, even though it had been
lovely. I told her we were fixing to make it legal as soon as we
could get on down to the city hall when it opened in the
morning. That shows you how much I knew afore the sun rose
on an awesome mess.

As we stood on the outside landing by the dawn's early light
we found we could still look one another in the eye after all,
and we had to kiss some more to celebrate the sheer wonder of
our still being able to. As near as we ever figured, the simple
but sturdy structure had been tie-bolted good to a foundation of
well-mortared sandstone blocks instead of bricks. Here and
there another building stood lonesome, but for at least two
blocks to each side of the now-deeper channel, there was
mostly windrows of shattered, mud-coated timbers and siding,
with a stove pipe here and a human limb there, sticking up out
of the wreckage.

Folk who were still moving were starting to pick through the
soggy debris by now. I kissed Martha again and told her, "I'll
be back as soon as all this allows, honey. You and your mother
made it. I got to see who else might have."

She wanted to go with me. I told her it was a fine notion to
get dressed, but that she'd best stay with her mother. Then I lit
out before she could argue.

By the time I made it to the water-filled hole where my
boardinghouse had once stood, the militia was out on the soggy
streets restoring order. I didn't see Colonel Chivington that
morning but I heard him from two streets over. A militiaman,
standing guard on a nearby mud-caked bank vault, told me
they had orders to shoot any looters on sight. I assured him
looting was not half as important to me as my job.

When I made it as far as the tannery I saw I didn't have no job. Later, I learned, some of the vats fetched up way out on the prairie to be used as cattle watering tanks. Nobody knows to this day whatever happened to the tannery owners, who'd lived nearby in a low-slung house with plastered sod walls.

Getting back to Martha and her mother took longer. The wreckage-littered streets were more crowded, and militiamen kept stopping me to ask who I was and where I thought I was going. Some of them knew me. Most of 'em had joined up since Glorieta, judging from the Roman numeral III on their hat badges. The "Bloodless Third" was a mite sensitive about the grander rep of the Colorado Firsters, and that seemed to make 'em officious as hell, even for part-time soldiers. I passed this one old boy halfway up a leaning telegraph pole. Before the militia had strung him up, they'd hung a pasteboard sign on his chest. It read, "CAUGHT LOOTING!" and that's likely why I didn't see anyone looting anything, all the way back to the notions shop.

Now in broad day I naturally had a look-see down into the shop. Getting in was easy enough. The glass was all gone. Everything inside was coated with cowshit-colored mud. What there *was*, I mean. The counters had piled up against the back wall, too big to be swept out the back door and windows. Some shelves still clung to the walls. Here and there you could make out a spool of thread or a card of buttons in the crud all over the floor. But most of the stock was just gone, and what was left had been ruined.

Knowing the 'dobe soil of Denver sets almost as hard as plaster, once it dries, I picked up a loose length of siding and commenced to shovel muck out the shattered front door. Martha must have heard me, and hoping I wasn't a looter, came down to take a look, holding a broom in one hand and her late father's horse pistol in the other. Her skirts were knotted betwixt her bare legs to keep the hems out of the muck. Her soft brown hair hung down unpinned as if she was ready to go to bed. I know I was, but I said, "I told you I'd be back. Things are worse, downstream. The place I used to work is gone. So's

the boardinghouse I used to stay. It's a good thing we're fixing
to get hitched, ain't it?''

She smiled weakly and replied, ''If only, dear heart. I meant
every word I said, upstairs in the dark, but my mother just
won't stand for it before I'm of age.''

I scooped out more muck and muttered, ''We live in changing times, and lots of folks are going to have to change their
minds about a heap of things before it's over. I'm moving in
with you, here. Both you gals need a man around the house till
things get back to sensible. If she'd rather see us living in sin,
so be it.''

Martha laughed more sincerely and allowed I had a convincing way of putting things. Then she sighed and added,
''We're liable to worry more about our empty stomachs than
our morals, now. Everything Mother and me had to call our
own was tied up in this shop, and I don't see anything left that
we could ask a penny for, do you?''

I said, ''Hard to tell, till we tidy up a mite. It might make
more sense to start all over with a man's saddle shop instead of
a ladies notion shop, here. We wouldn't have to put things
back together quite as dainty, leather goods sell for way more
than buttons and bows, and I know how to cut, stitch, and tool
leather.''

I scooped more muck, catching sight of the floorboards for
a moment this time, and went on, ''I know leather, too. The
trick to working it is picking the right heft and surface for what
you want to make. I know plenty of old boys in the tanning
trade and they couldn't have *all* drowned last night. So once
we get this place mucked out and put back together a mite I'll
just pick up the stuff I'll need and—''

''With what?'' she cut in. Women are more practical than us
about a heap of things, no matter how they carry on whilst
we're taking cruel advantage of them. She put her dad's gun
down and started sweeping, even as she insisted it was useless.
She said that betwixt stocking the shop, and the payments on
the building to the city as well as the bank, there was simply
no way the three of us would be able to manage on the few
dollars we had left between us.

I nodded and said, "I know. I'm going to have to borrow a thousand or more from some bank, if I can find one still in business."

She said, "Ross, you big silly, you don't have any security, and even if you did you're not old enough. Don't you have to be twenty-one to vote or borrow money from a bank?"

I shrugged and said, "Let's not tell 'em, then. I'm still one of the heroes of Glorieta Pass, and if that won't do it I don't know what will."

Glorieta Pass did it. Turner & Bobs had survived both the fire and flood, which was more than a heap of their previous clients could say. I suspect they were anxious for new business. They never asked how old I was and said they'd be proud to lend me a couple of thousand at twenty-five percent a month. So I said I might try Wells Fargo, and they came down to ten percent, which was bad enough but what the hell. I figured that if I didn't have any money coming in by the time I'd paid half the loan back as interest, we'd be out of business in any case.

But as things panned out, Turner & Bobs only made six hundred dollars in usury afore I was able to pay 'em off in full by late summer. Once I got to doing it serious I found I had a knack for working leather, and Martha said I owed some of our fame along Larimer to my personality. That was what she called giving the customer what they wanted—personality. It was just as easy to cut a gun or sword belt so's it hung the way the customer fancied, and did a cowhand want a design I found silly tooled into his *buscadero* rig or saddle skirts, it was him, not me, who'd be admired or teased by his pals.

We got a heap of business from the Colorado Volunteers, once word got about that one of their old scouts was ready to repair busted harness or even make you new gear, cheap. Colonel Chivington was an early customer and, better yet, when I told him Martha and me had just been married civil in the temporary City Hall—a circus tent—the preaching militant said he'd be proud to treat us to a military wedding of the Methodist persuasion.

Martha had been dunked a Baptist whilst I'd been sprinkled

Scotch Presbyterian, but we took the colonel up on his kind
offer so's my Martha could make a mighty handsome June
bride in her mother's old wedding dress, with me gussied up in
borrowed army blue. I have to say the Colorado Volunteers did
us proud.

Since the regular Methodist church had been swept away by
the flood, the colonel borrowed Saint Mary's for the occasion
off Father Machelbuef, a good sport of the Papist persuasion.
The nice old priest and his nuns were a big help when Martha's
mother was overcome and had to be revived with smelling
salts. They wanted to have a priest with medical training look
her over more serious but she just laughed, sort of sheepish,
and said it had only been the thrill of seeing her only child
come down them steps under all them crossed swords.

She seemed all right at the reception they threw for us at the
Tremont House. Later on, once I'd changed back into my
civilian duds and loaded both ladies in our buggie to get 'em on
home, the boys still gave us a mounted escort all the way. But,
having said all them nice things about the Colorado Volunteers, I have to record that some of 'em, at least, were mighty
slow when it came to paying their bills. It sounded sort of
unpatriotic to refuse a trooper credit for new taps or a fancy,
albeit not regulation martingale, but I had my own creditors to
pay and by fall I was really taking a beating. So I rode over one
afternoon to ask Colonel Chivington what was up.

I had to go through a snotty sergeant major to get in to see
the colonel, but once I did Chivington acted friendly as ever.
He set me in a horsehair chair and offered me a two-bit cigar
from the fancy humidor atop his big desk, even though he
never smoked, his ownself. He said he was glad to see me but
that I should have shown up sooner, afore the *News* had published the proposed reforms to the Conscription Acts. He said,
"Governor Evans has frozen our table of organization, and
he's simply not signing any more militia commissions until
things are settled one way or the other back east, Clark. But we
might be able to work our way around the restrictions for a
veteran of the New Mexico Campaign."

I must have looked as confused as his words had left me. For the colonel frowned with his big bushy brows and demanded, "You did come to see me about your draft status, didn't you, son?"

I shook my head and replied, "Nosir. Nobody mentioned the draft to me when they held the first drawings a month or so back. I reckon you have to be old enough to vote afore they figure you're old enough to draft into the army. Or mayhaps they figure, since I've already done my part in this fool war—"

"Your civilian scouting contract cuts no ice with the paper-pushers at the new draft office," the colonel cut in, adding, "don't look at *me* that way, son. I know you saw more action with us down around Santa Fe than many an infantry private may ever see under sluggards such as McClellan or Meade. But Washington's running scared since the draft riots they had last July. They'll be bending over backwards to make the next one seem more fair. Each district has a quota of soldiers to provide. If they can't recruit enough volunteers by way of bounties and mayhaps the county jails, up to twenty percent of the able-bodied men in the district will be drafted by lottery. They likely missed you this summer because you hadn't registered to vote, yet. When *will* you be old enough to vote the straight Republican ticket, Son?"

I muttered, numbly, "Just afore Easter, Colonel, but see here, I got me a wife and a mother-in-law to support and didn't I hear somewheres a man could buy his way outten the fool draft when and if all else failed?"

Colonel Chivington nodded grimly and replied, "What did you think those shanty Irish back east were rioting about last July? Tell a mill worker with a wife and seven children that he's off to fight the boys in butternut gray because he hasn't got the cash to buy his own commutation fee and I'll show you a Paddy with a brick in one hand and a pick handle in the other!"

He leaned back in his own chair and added, "They're still taking commutation cash and allowing draftees to furnish their own substitutes. They do need the money, after all. But you can still be called up in the very next draft, and guess whose names go to the head of the list?"

I said, "Well, if being married up don't count, and being a

fool who's already fought don't count, I reckon I'll just have
to cross my fingers and hope they don't draw my name from
the drum afore this war wears down. What I really came to
bitch about is past-due bills for leather work I've done for your
outfit, Colonel.''

He asked for more details. I produced a sheaf of orders I'd
never been paid for and handed 'em over. Colonel Chivington
didn't seem too surprised by some of the new names. He
growled, ''Leave these with me and I'll see you're paid, son.
This is what *I've* been bitching about to the political machine
that hands out commissions so freely, and I've been *looking* for
an excuse to bounce some of these worthless draft-dodgers.''

He set the bills aside with a sigh and added, ''We're not
talking about the outfit you may recall from the time we rode
together down New Mexico way, Ross. Thanks to the Conscription Acts passed last spring you've no idea how many
sissies with friends in high places have elected to serve in our
fine part-time militia.''

I said, ''No I wouldn't. I've been stuck for a heap of sword
belts and fancy saddle skirts, Colonel.''

Chivington stared past me, or through me, to say half to
himself, ''If only there was some *action* to occupy so many of
them, even part-time. The war department's kicked up a fuss
about our calling up three whole regiments in such otherwise
empty country. So we have to cull out some of the deadwood.
But how do you separate good fighting men from bad when
Texas doesn't want to fight you anymore and . . . Never mind.
Let's talk about your draft status, son.''

I said, ''I thought we already did, Colonel. If they call me
up I reckon I'll just have to go. I got a couple of neighborhood
kids helping out around the shop, and if push ever comes to
shove I reckon my Martha can run things till I get back, if I'm
lucky enough to get back, I mean.''

Colonel Chivington shook his head and said, ''I've a better
idea, Clark. The governor won't let me commission you and I
know you'd as soon have more free time than that in any case.
But what if I was to enlist you as a personal scout, with the
rank of, oh, I suppose we could get away with staff sergeant.''

I had to cock a brow and consider some before I answered.
For as young as I still was at the time, I'd already noticed that
when deals seemed too good to be true they likely were. I said,
"I'd surely hate to go back east and mayhaps shoot it out with
the neighbor boys from my parts of Tennessee, Colonel. But
how come you want to be so nice to me, seeing that, no
offense, you just now said you didn't have enough work for the
men you already have?"

The colonel opened a desk drawer and fumbled out a manila
folder filled with newspaper clippings. He handed one over. I
knew right off it was an editorial from a Democratic newspaper. It read:

### PROSPECT OF INDIAN TROUBLES

As our readers are well aware, our Arapaho and
Cheyenne neighbors are at about the same state with us
as the Santee Sioux under Little Crow were with the
whites of the Minnesota Valley at about this same time,
last year. A growing animosity to the white race has
been apparent since the outbreak of the War Between
the States because the savages can see all too clearly
that if they ever mean to reverse the Manifest Destiny
of this country . . .

I handed the rest back, softly saying, "The army rounded up
them Santee and hung a good many of 'em high, last winter,
Colonel. Are you saying you expect the Indians in these parts
to act that silly this fall? Jim Beckwourth tells me most of 'em
are holding their last big buffalo hunt of the year over to the
Smoky Hills about now. That'd put most of the bands a good
hundred and twenty miles from here, right?"

Chivington shrugged and said, "*Most* bands don't signify
*all* bands, and the Smoky Hills are still on our side of the
Colorado-Kansas line. I knew Black Kettle, Left Hand, and
Little Raven keep saying they just love us all to death and only
want to be left alone. Little Crow was saying much the same
just before the Sioux burnt two hundred houses and killed over

a hundred white men, women, and children at New Ulm Minnesota, around fall, wasn't it?''

I nodded but said, "Jim Beckwourth knows Indians way better than you or me, Colonel.''

Chivington smiled thinly and replied, "I know how well that old darky knows them, indeed. He tells me he's a blood brother to Leg In Water of the South Cheyenne, and that they've even given him his own Indian name, which translates something like Medicine Calf.''

I didn't like the way we seemed to be drifting and I said so, adding, "Colored or covered with feathers and paint, Jim Beckwourth's still a friend of mine, Colonel. As I recall, he rode with both of us through considerable cactus and cannon fire, down New Mexico way that time.''

Chivington assured me, soothingly, "Jim's personal honor is not in question, Clark! It's his judgment, not his loyalty, I can't help questioning when, well, questions keep coming up.''

I asked him to spell it out better.

He said, "You know I've always relied on Jim Beckwourth as my chief scout. I'm sure that he in turn has always done his best to serve as my eyes and ears in the field. But you have to admit Jim's awfully thick with the half-breed Bent brothers and that old squaw-man, John Smith.''

I nodded and said, "I've met Uncle John, as we call him, or Gray Blanket, as the Indians call him. It stands to reason Jim would want to compare notes with blood brothers, breeds, squaw-men and such. Who *else* is likely to tell you what the local Indians might be up to?''

Chivington stared down at the papers atop his desk the way a little kid might stare at a plate of spinach as he muttered, "I wonder what they call John Smith's Indian squaw, Pocahontas? You know that can't be the old man's real name, don't you?''

I shrugged and replied, "Mayhaps he ain't proud of being an old squaw-man with a drinker's nose, Colonel. If Jim trusts his word on more important matters, that's good enough for me.''

"It's not good enough for me," said Chivington, adding,

"I'm in command of too many troops to grope in the dark, and that's all I'm doing with one so-called expert assuring me the Indians are dear little lambs while yet another warns me they're about to go on the infernal war path any infernal minute! I need a scout who thinks for himself. It could be to both our advantage if you were to enlist as my personal, ah . . . How shall we put it?"

I grimaced and started to suggest "Teacher's Pet," but stopped. I wanted him to get those deadbeats of his to pay the damned bills they owed us. So I said I'd think it over.

I did, too. But nobody else got drafted out our way for the rest of the year, and the first early frosts did send most of the Arapaho and South Cheyenne into winter camps amongst the cottonwood draws of the Smoky Hills, way off the east where they couldn't bother nobody and vice versa. Meanwhile business picked up at the saddle shop and my mother-in-law was laid low with more of them fainting spells. So I just forgot about the war, Mr. Lo, and such for a spell.

Martha's mother lasted long enough to finish the muffler she'd been knitting me for my birthday. Then she died, as if to prove she hadn't just been putting on them fainting spells. I felt bad about it, too. But it was a neighbor woman who pointed out to Martha that being married up didn't cut no ice with the draft board unless a man could show he had kids or aging kin to support who'd starve without him. Martha allowed she didn't see how she'd ever produce us enough kids to matter before they held the next draft, albeit I have to say she was a good sport about *trying*. The same expert on the subject said I'd be foolish to register to vote, now that I could, because they got the names for the draft drums off the local voting lists. Martha said she understood when I allowed there was no sense living in a free country unless you got to vote the rascals who run it in or out. So I just went and registered my fool self to vote that fall and as luck would have it my name wasn't called in the spring draft of '64.

I'd naturally told Martha about Colonel Chivington wanting me to act as some sort of snoop. She agreed a man would have to be mighty low to tattle on his pals, but she asked if I was sure that was exactly what the colonel wanted me to do for him. She said she kept hearing all kinds of tales about Indian troubles, and that it was surely a good thing we lived smack in town and didn't have to worry about Mr. Lo as much as some, because it was awfully tough to tell who was right or wrong when Chicken Little kept saying the sky was falling.

Whether you feel Mr. Lo had a just beef with the U.S. Government or not, nobody can accuse the American Indian of being too dumb to see a chance and take advantage of it. The war back east was building to an all out bloodbath, with Grant in command of all the Union forces now and anxious to pull off a big win before the fall elections.

Lee, in turn, was just as aware McClellan was fixing to run against Lincoln on a peace platform. So he was busting a gut to bloody Grant in the Wilderness Campaign and you didn't have to read the *Washington Post* to see the western army posts were now about as undermanned as they ever figured to get.

I've already mentioned the Great Sioux Uprising to our northeast. To our southwest a young officer called Rope Thrower by the Indians and Colonel Kit Carson by everyone else was having a bitch of a time with the Navaho, Mescaleros, and such.

Opinion remained divided, mighty divided, on the Arapaho and South Cheyenne closer to Denver. Jim Beckwourth opined a heap of the proddy tales were inspired by most of the bands favoring the swell hunting grounds directly east of town, athwart the main post road and wagon trace betwixt Denver and Kansas City. The Smoky Hills weren't really what we'd have called hills, back home in Tennessee. Near the Kansas-Colorado line the headwaters of, say, half a dozen seasonal streams had cut a big but otherwise gentle rise into a monster-some stretch of rolling prairie laced with deep brushy draws, just made for the lifestyle of the Plains Indian. Crossing such country by stage or covered wagon made most whites proddy as hell. For whilst it seemed as if one could see for miles across all that tawny grass you could stumble over whole villages of Indian lodges in most any draw, with the lodge poles and even a good bit of the smoke hidden below the general level of the open range.

Jim Beckwourth, old John Smith, and others who felt less proddy in the company of Mr. Lo, kept saying none of the sagamores, or big chiefs of the Arapaho and South Cheyenne, wanted any trouble. When, now and again, trouble happened anyways, Jim said that just went with having Indians in the same country with you. Some of our own young rascals could be pains in the ass as well when they got the chance to help themselves to an Indian's pony, squaw, or whatever. Jim allowed a red or white man who'd really done something awful deserved to be punished. But, as he agreed as soon as I pointed it out to him and young George Bent in the Jayhawker one evening, Indians were no more anxious to turn their wilder kids over to us for punishment than we were to hand a drunken cowhand over to Cheyenne dog soldiers after he'd had a little fun with one of their squaws.

Since this comes up now and again, and George Bent was sitting there agreeing with us, even though his mother had been a Cheyenne squaw called Yellow Woman, I'd best point out that unlike Sioux, Shoshone, and such, neither Cheyenne nor Arapaho got insulted when you called one of their women a squaw. It just means "woman" in their Algonquin dialects and, while I had young Bent on the subject, I asked and got him to agree his mama's people had learned to scalp folk without any help from wicked white men. Cheyenne were notorious, even by Indian standards, for scalping very thoroughly. George said they mutilated the hands of dead enemies as well, to give themselves the edge if they ever met up with 'em again as ghosts in, say, a dream. George said most Indians held dreams to be real visits to the Spirit World and I wasn't about to argue with old George. He was the breed son of little White Man or William Bent, one of the brothers who'd built Old Bent's Fort where the Santa Fe Trail crosses the Arkansas well south of Denver. Since he played a part in this story, later on, I may as well add that George had two breed sisters and two more breed brothers, since Little White Man had married up with Cheyenne ladies called Owl Woman and Yellow

Woman. Jim Beckwourth told me, later, George and his one
brother, Charlie, spent more time with the Indians than the rest
of the family because Yellow Woman had packed up and gone
home to her own band after an argument with her white hus-
band about our way of doing business. Yellow Woman held it
was mighty mean-spirited to deny all her kith and kin trade
goods just because they couldn't pay for 'em.

I was tempted to tell Jim Beckwourth about the colonel
trying to get me to check up on him and his Indian pals. I never
said anything, for two reasons. I felt no call to betray the
colonel's confidence unless I meant to go along with his fool
talk about Indian troubles and, as winter gave way to green-up,
it got ever tougher to determine just who might be talking the
most foolish.

For there *was* Indian trouble, albeit neither side seemed able
to agree on just what had happened, once the gunsmoke
cleared.

Some militia riders from the Firsters brushed with a party of
South Cheyenne they found in the company of some stolen
horses, and two troopers were killed in the resulting hoedown.
Major Jacob Downing of the Colorado Volunteers tracked the
killers to the nearest Cheyenne camp, he said, and attacked at
daybreak, losing one more man and killing at least two dozen
Indians. The Indians said Downing had attacked the wrong
band. He for certain had killed some women and children. He
allowed as much in his report, pointing out how tough it is to
attack a horse thief at home without involving his kith and kin.

Nobody ever explained to either side's satisfaction how an
elderly South Cheyenne called Lean Bear managed to get himself killed by the regular army. According to Jim Beckwourth,
who got the Indian's side of the story, Lean Bear had been a
not-too-bright but curious cuss regarded more for his *matou*, or
medicine, than any deep thought he'd ever displayed. During
a visit to an army post Lean Bear had noticed a swell shiny ring
on the dainty finger of an army officer's wife. He'd asked her,
in Tsitsissah, to let him try in on for size and, when that hadn't
worked, he'd just grabbed the white lady's hand to pry it off
her, inspiring some mighty fine screaming on the part of the

officer's wife and a good lick alongside the head from the officer's riding crop.

Lean Bear had gone home and put on his feathers and paint. But cooler heads had prevailed until later, in the month of May, Lean Bear and some other Indians had met up with a mounted patrol near Ash Creek, and Lean Bear rode forward to assure the soldiers of his band's good intent, according to the Indians. According to the U.S. Army soldiers, the Indian had charged at them.

In either event, that had been the end of Lean Bear and an all-out battle had been prevented by a powwow after both sides had taken a few more casualties.

There were other such skirmishes, neither side willing to admit anyone they knew had fired the first shot. A serious amount of stock was run off down by Coal Creek, by Indians, according to the whites, or by white thieves, according to the Indians, when asked.

But there has never been any doubt who was in the wrong when a total son of a bitch led fellow members of the Cheyenne Crooked Lance Society to a remote little cattle spread twenty-odd miles south of Denver. For Martha and me knew the white family butchered there.

Nat Hungate and his pretty young wife, Ellen, were raising cows and kids along Running Creek on range Nat had leased from a bigger stockman named Van Wormer. Martha had met Ellen Hungate a spell back, when Martha and her mother had still been selling ladies notions downstairs. The Hungates came in to shop every other month, weather permitting. Ellen had bought ribbon bows for her two daughters, little Florence, six, and tiny Laura, three years old.

Nat and Ellen Hungate were decent folk who'd never had any trouble with anybody, red or white. Their landlord, Van Wormer, was considered a tolerable cuss as well.

But, as well as anyone was ever able to put the sad story together, Nat Hungate and a hired hand called Miller were up the creek a piece, hunting for a stray calf, when they noticed smoke rising from the sod house in the distance. Hungate ordered young Miller to ride like the wind for help. Then, like a fool, or a worried father, he rode on in to see what he could do for Ellen and his girls.

He couldn't do much. When Miller got back with Van Wormer and enough help to matter, they found what was left of Nat Hungate in his dooryard, punctured eighty times with lance tips and missing his scalp, the fingers of his right hand, and his privates.

It took the irate cowhands longer to locate Ellen and the two little girls. Their naked, mutilated bodies had been stuffed down the well. The three of 'em, including tiny Laura, had been gang-raped and scalped.

All four bodies had been loaded aboard a spring wagon and trucked into Denver where, draped more modest, they'd been placed on display in the window of a furniture store.

I didn't want Martha to come along for a look-see, but you know how women are. After she'd puked all down the front of my work shirt she recovered herself, and allowed she was surely sorry and that she'd get me into a fresh shirt if only I'd take her home now.

I told her not to worry about that, as I led her off gentle. When she said I'd surely want to put on another shirt I told her, "I know. I had an Army Blue shirt in mind."

So she just said, "Oh," and never raised a fuss.

I told you I fell for Martha because she was smart as well as pretty.


The First Colorado was maintained at full strength all through the war years. The Second Colorado was more a headquarters and service unit. In response to the howl that went up over the Hungates, Governor Evans got his cheap territorial government to authorize and fund the Third Colorado at full regimental strength for at least a hundred days. Colonel Chivington allowed that if he couldn't round up the infernal South Cheyenne and Arapaho combined, in a hundred days, he'd resign his commission as a proven fool.

I barely got to talk to the colonel when I reported in to track down Indians for him. But his offer proved to be still good for the staff sergeant's rating he'd offered and, since he didn't repeat his fool request I spy on Jim Beckwourth on the sly, I figured he'd about decided to forget it. Like I said, I was still young in them days.

On the face of it Colonel Chivington had no call to suspect Jim Beckwourth of covering up for his Indian pals, as we all got set to go out after Indians. If anything, old Jim was pissed at Mr. Lo more than anybody, and everybody was mighty pissed.

Jim had this arrow shaft someone had brung in from the Hungate spread, and he kept telling anyone who'd listen that the blue medicine stripes on the crow feather-vaned shaft not only read Cheyenne but South Cheyenne of the Crooked Lance Society. Young Miller had been chased partway to the Van Wormer spread by a cuss waving a lance at him, whether crooked or straight, and when he recalled the Indian's peculiar war paint Jim swore and said, "I knew it! Motavato's told me personal there's just no talking sense to that ornery Woquina when he's feeling adventuresome!"

I had to agree anyone who'd paint his forehead chrome yellow, his nose and cheekbones tomato-red, and his chin black as soot didn't sound too sensible. But I'd still never heard of any rascals with such dispronounceable names.

To which Jim replied, "Sure you have. We call Motavato Black Kettle in English, and Woquina's better knowed to us as Roman Nose because he's part white with the profile of a Greek god."

Jim spat and added, "You got to watch Horse Indians with white blood. Roman Nose first counted coup way back in the Battle of the Solomon, and they say young Quanah Parker's meaner than half his Comanche kin!"

"Like George and Charlie Bent?" I couldn't help asking.

Jim had sense enough to laugh, sheepish, and point out, "The Bent boys ain't the same. Old Bill Bent's a trader as likes pretty squaws, not a captive white gal forced to nurse her babies in a tipi. George and Charlie act like everyone else—when they ain't off hunting with their Cheyenne cousins, least-ways."

I said that, either way, the colonel would want to know it

was old Roman Nose we were after, and not the main bands
over to the Smoky Hills. So we tracked him down and told him
about the medicine paint Miller had noticed near the Hungate
spread. The colonel listened with polite enough interest but
decided, "We can separate the sheep from the goats after we
round up the whole herd. How many hostiles are we likely to
meet in the Smoky Hills, Jim?"

The grizzled maroon was not a man to guess at numbers
when he didn't know 'em. He simply replied, "Hard to say. I
suspect there's always more coyotes and fewer Indians skulk-
ing about than most whites ought to worry about. The Bureau
of Indian Affairs figures the South Cheyenne have forty-odd
sagamores leading as many bands. There ain't half that many
Arapaho."

Colonel Chivington nodded and said, "Let me see if I have
this straight. A sagamore is a high chief, a sachem is a sub-
chief who might lead a buffalo hunt or war party, while a
pinasee is a warrior who's counted coup and rates feathers and
a say around the council fire, right?"

When Jim nodded, Chivington smiled thinly and repeated
his question about hostiles in the Smoky Hills. Jim spat and
replied, "Can't even say how many of 'em might be *hostiles*,
damn it. Black Kettle's band is big as they come, and leave us
not forget at least three outten four will be women and children."

Chivington said, tight-lipped, "I don't mean to forget that
ratio. They butchered one man, one woman, and two babies at
the Hungate spread. How much time do you think I have to
work with? Half our new recruits don't know which end of the
gun the bullet comes out of. Do you think we have at least a
few weeks to whip our punitive expedition into shape?"

Jim Beckwourth shrugged and answered, "Depends on Mr.
Lo. By now he'll be expecting us. They call them rises the
Smoky Hills because you see so many smoke signals as you
follow the post road east to Kansas. They'll have already
headed for Kansas themselves, if they mean what they say
about not wanting an all-out with us. If they *do* want one, I
can't think of a better place to make a stand if I was Mr. Lo.

The Smoky Hills offers a heap of game, water, firewood, and a swampsome number of ideal ambush sites. So if I was you I'd want to offer my green troopers more than a few weeks training, Colonel. Some of them crooked-lancers have been fighting us, good, since the first covered wagon come over their horizon! Like I said, Roman Nose won his first coup feather fighting J.E.B. Stuart when that rebel son of a bitch was still on *our* side. It's pure murder to send a kid with less than six or eight weeks training into a firefight, and he's still up Shit Creek if he meets up with someone like Roman Nose in the field. That handsome butcher trails forty coup feathers in the tail of his war bonnet, and they don't grant you a coup feather for every old boy you kill. You got to do it crazy-mean, agin odds.''

Chivington sniffed and said, ''I'm aware they consider war some sort of children's game. If you're sure they won't run off from the Smoky Hills, in less than six or eight weeks we'll be in shape to really show the rascals how the game is played!''

Jim grimaced and said, ''If they ain't run off already, I doubt they will this side of the big fall buffalo hunts. For there ain't a much better place to harvest buff than the Smoky Hills.''

Chivington nodded thoughtfully and said, ''The scattered bands usually gather in handy bunches during the fall hunting season, don't they?''

Jim nodded soberly and said, ''Yep. As good a time to hunt buffalo, or Indians, as I can think of. Of course, it all depends on how many buffalo rounds they might still have left when first they notice our arrival on the scene!''

I had to laugh when my name was drawn in the second draft of '64. They couldn't take me because I was already a staff sergeant in the militia and listed on active duty to boot, even though I only had to traipse out to Camp Weld now and again to make sure the outfit was still there. As a scout, even though they'd listed me as a militant, nobody expected me to do anything all that military.

Knowing that sooner or later we might be moving out against Mr. Lo, I gave young Tim O'Connel a raise and put him in charge of the routine repairs and such in the back, leaving it up to Martha to take orders and make changes out front whenever I had to be away.

As time wore on and all they did out at the camp was dismounted drill and target practice, I got to feeling a mite silly about the fancy blue blouse with yaller stripes and left it hanging on the wall most of the time. I saw by the papers that General Pope had the Sioux under control in Minnesota, whilst Kit Carson had cowed the Apache and cornered the Navaho down amid the canyonlands of Arizona Territory. I found the war back east and the coming elections way more interesting. Old U.S. Grant had sent Sherman marching through Georgia to convince all concerned that War was Hell, and while the papers failed to say what pool old Hannibal Hamlin had done to make his party sore at him, I saw they were running Andrew Johnson of Tennessee to be the vice-president if Lincoln won a second term. I told Martha that left me in a quandary indeed. For while I figured Honest Abe had done as well as could be expected, folk back home said Johnson could talk more and say less than any white man who'd ever drawn breath and sipped corn betwixt the Blue Ridge and the Muddy Mississippi, Martha said she'd heard you didn't have to vote for every name on the ticket, and I had to agree with her that some gals, at least, had just as much sense and ought to have as much right to vote as half the men-folk we knew.

Then, just as the kids were fixing to go back to school in Denver and the Colorado Volunteers were fixing to march out against Mr. Lo, the regular army dealt Colonel Chivington a distressing blow indeed.

I mean, here we were, up to full strength with plenty of powder, caps, and balls, mess kits shiny, sabers sharpened, and a change of socks and underwear for everybody, when Major Edward Wynkoop and around a hundred mounted regulars out of Fort Lyon accepted the surrender of all the bands in the Smoky Hills without a fight.

I could hardly blame Colonel Chivington for taking it so personal, after the newspapers got through writing it up so

comical. They named a downtown street in Denver after Wynkoop, later, and nobody can say he didn't rate the honor. For
Tall Chief Wynkoop, as the Indians called him, was slated for
a long career as first an army officer and later a firm but fair
Indian agent during some even tenser times with Mr. Lo before
things finally simmered down after Wounded Knee.

But, at the time he stole Colonel Chivington's thunder, Ed
Wynkoop was only a couple of years older than Martha and
me. He'd made his oak leaves fighting under Canby down in
New Mexico, that time the regulars lost Santa Fe to the rebs
and the Colorado Volunteers had to save their bacon. So you
can imagine how Chivington and his senior officers felt about
it when young Major Wynkoop announced he was bringing the
principal Cheyenne and Arapaho chiefs into Denver for a powwow with Governor Evans to settle all this bull, once and for
all.

Tall Chief Wynkoop and his modest force of mounted troopers force-marched eight sagamores and, more amazingly, four
white captives he'd rescued, into Denver around the end of
September. The whole town turned out for the spectacle. The
Indians rode in one army ambulance or spring wagon used for
general transportation. The four rescued whites, all kids, got to
ride a mite fancier, albeit Black Kettle had mounted a big
garrison flag over his own plank seat to indicate he was an
American Indian, which he was, fair enough, as soon as you
study on it. He and some of the others sported those silver
medals Washington kept handing out to chiefs for some fool
reason. Black Kettle, White Antelope, Bull Bear, and Ochinee
(or One-Eye) were there to speak for the South Cheyenne.
Heaps-of-Buffalo, Bosse, Neva, and Notanee were there to
speak for the Arapaho. Roman Nose of the South Cheyenne
and Little Raven of the Arapaho didn't seem to want to jaw
with Governor Evans. Left Hand of the Arapaho had allowed
he'd stay behind and keep his own band from taking Fort Lyon
whilst Tall Chief was away on business.

The first business Governor Evans brought up, at Colonel
Chivington's suggestion, was those four white kids kidnapped
by the infernal Cheyenne.

Black Kettle explained that two white women and five children had been captured up along the South Platte by some other Indians. He said he knew this might make the Great White Father angry and so he'd ransomed the four younger kids with his own ponies. He just couldn't say what might have happened to the two grown women and one young gal, after that. Major Wynkoop horned in to say he'd interviewed the four youngsters he had found in Black Kettle's possession and that they'd all assured him they'd been treated tolerable by the second band they'd been held by.

Governor Evans wanted to know who'd treated the Hungate children way less gentle. Black Kettle looked pained and said he'd heard about that and agreed it was wrong to rape and murder three-year-olds. When he suggested that had likely been the work of Sioux, it was Jim Beckwourth's turn to step forward and cuss them all out in their own lingo. Colonel Chivington didn't savvy Tsitsissah but he still nodded and said, "Sioux stripe their arrow shafts with red medicine paint, not blue, as the Cheyenne shafts stuck in Nat Hungate were striped. There are no Sioux south of Denver in any case. You lying savages know as well as we do that it was Roman Nose and his crooked-lancers who committed that outrage!"

Black Kettle ignored him. That really made Colonel Chivington feel fond as hell of Indians in general. Old White Antelope looked as if he was fixing to cry as he stepped forward, patting the silver medal on his skinny brown chest as he half chanted and half sobbed, "Hear me! Maybe it was Woquina who did bad things to those little white girls. Maybe it was somebody else. I was not there. None of us, here, were there. But hear me, I *was* there when men who said they spoke for the Great White Father called us all up to Fort Laramie to speak of peace. I was there when, after there was no peace, we all went down to Fort Larned to make peace with Colonel Greenwood. We got these medals. We got the big American flag my brother, Motavato, here, still has. But where is the *peace* you people keep promising us?"

Colonel Chivington snorted in disgust and snapped, "Peace

is not a one-way street, White Antelope. When you shoot at us, we shoot at you. It's as simple as that.''

Black Kettle wailed, ''You people always shoot first! Don't we have any right to protect ourselves?''

Chivington started to ask, real sarcastic, whether it had been Florence or Laura Hungate who'd menaced Roman Nose the most that time. But Doc Evans held up a hand for silence and said, ''We could go on all day about who did what, with what, to whom, and we'd still be arguing about it when the cows came home. So here's what I think we'd best all agree to in hopes that *this* time, damn it, there'll be no misunderstandings between our two breeds.''

The governor must have already been thinking ahead. For he'd had it all put down on paper before the meeting and I, for one, thought his notion made sense.

The Arkansas River ran more or less west to east about a hundred-odd miles south of Denver. In them days there hadn't been much in the way of white settlement down yonder. Sand Creek, a deep-timbered draw, ran south into the Arkansas at a forty-five-degree angle. The two met just inside the Colorado-Kansas line, enclosing a big triangle of varied range, mostly rolling prairie, with Fort Lyon at about the center of the bottom line, along the Arkansas. Governor Evans pointed out that the Indians would have a reserve of around two thousand square miles if they agreed to behave themselves down yonder, ranging no farther east than Sand Creek or west of, say, Horse Creek, with the troops and Indian agency at Fort Lyon keeping an eye on all concerned, red or white.

Black Kettle didn't like it as much as Doc Evans and me. He said the hunting was way better up in the Smoky Hills, northeast of upper Sand Creek. The Arapaho complained they liked to hunt south of the Arkansas now and again. Colonel Chivington snorted that the governor was offering way more than they deserved and that if they'd rather fight it was jake with him.

They must have figured he meant it. I know I did, having followed the cuss off a cliff one time. Young Major Wynkoop helped by promising the army would feed 'em if the hunting turned out bad as Motavato feared. So after some more jawing back and forth the eight sagamores allowed they might get by on a patch of Colorado big enough to qualify as a state of its own right along the eastern seaboard. White Antelope said he'd made such deals before and asked Doc Evans to put it all in writing. I suspect White Antelope was a mite surprised to have Colonel Chivington agree with him.

The colonel said, "The South Cheyenne alone recognize forty-odd sagamores. I only see four here, Governor. What do you propose we cede the *others* when the army takes *their* scalping knives away?"

Major Wynkoop pointed out that Black Kettle was the paramount chief of his nation. Then he made the mistake of trying to prove it by bringing up the four white children Black Kettle had rescued from more truculent Indians.

Chivington snorted like an old bull with a fly betwixt its horns and growled, "You're being way too modest, Major. You and your own mounted regulars rescued those particular captives when you found them—I repeat, found them—in Black Kettle's possession when you rode into his camp, a good two days' ride from Fort Lyon."

Wynkoop looked uncomfortable and tried, "These gents were trying to arrange an exchange of prisoners through young George Bent when, to be frank, I thought it best to just go get 'em. I have a signed statement from young Ambrose Archer, the eldest of the captives, in which he states he rather enjoyed his stay with the Indians."

Chivington looked disgusted and replied, "When I was eight years old I liked to play Indian in the Ohio woods, too. What about those two white women, and the older girl we can assume to have been a virgin when they rode off with her? If Black Kettle speaks for all the lesser chiefs why can't he even tell us where those three poor white girls are, right now, being treated so grand by their captors?"

Jim Beckwourth chimed in, "Ask him how come Roman Nose ain't here, or Little Raven, or Left Hand. Nobody never accused any of *these* fine gents of lifting hair or horses all that recent. What sense is a peace treaty unless you get the ones who've been doing all the fighting to sign it?"

Governor Evans held up a hand for silence and declared, "This meeting is only an informal attempt at a pro tem cease fire. I don't have the authority to speak for the U.S. Government or even the Bureau of Indian Affairs. I'm only an appointed official, serving at the pleasure of the president, and who's to say who that might be after the elections, less than six weeks off?"

Turning to the Indians he said, "If you don't want to fight us anymore, right now, you'd best take all your people down to Fort Lyon where Major Wynkoop, here, and your Indian agent, Mr. Colley, can keep an eye on you. After my people decide who the Great White Father is going to be for the next four summers we can draw up a formal treaty and map out the exact limits of your grand reservation."

Black Kettle protested that the hunting down near Fort Lyon was poor. He said both the soldiers from the fort and settlers along the Arkansas had scared off all the game they hadn't actually shot.

Black Kettle said the two main traders down yonder, Little White Man and Gray Blanket, were honest enough but disinclined to offer credit, even when a man had no more buffalo robes but a lodge full of hungry kids to feed. Jim Beckwourth explained they were bitching about William Bent and the more mysterious John Smith.

Governor Evans repeated, and Major Wynkoop agreed, that should all else fail, the army would issue enough corned beef and flour to see everyone through the winter.

Colonel Chivington scowled and said, "With all due respect, sir, aren't you just robbing Peter to pay Paul? The Indians are right about the number of settlers moving onto that range you're being sort of generous with. President Lincoln signed that Homestead Act about the same time he freed the darkies and—"

"I said it was a pro tem stopgap," Doc Evans cut in, adding in a lower voice, "you eat any apple a bite at a time, and you get through this sort of business a winter at a time, if you're lucky."

Chivington growled, "What if we're *not* lucky, sir? What if we have a mild winter and these boys get to feeling frisky again?''

The governor shrugged and said, "Well, I raised your Third Colorado to fight Indians, didn't I?"

So half the Arapaho and South Cheyenne went on down to winter near Fort Lyon, well out of sight but hardly out of mind, for a heap of folk, not just in Denver, felt Mr. Lo had gotten off mighty easy after such a sullen summer. The opposition papers had a lot of fun with the poor old "Hundred Dazers" or "Bloodless Third," as they openly accused Governor Evans of providing a haven for draft-dodgers by bloating the Colorado Volunteers to fight Indians and then not fighting Indians worth spit.

The regular army seemed to think Major Wynkoop had acted sort of sissy, too. From Fort Leavenworth, General Samuel R. Curtis wired his own two cents' worth, demanding to know where in thunder those three captive white ladies might be right now, with whom, and accusing poor Wynkoop of exceeding his authority by taking his own captives up to Denver instead of, damn it, handing them over to the provost marshal to deal with as Little Crow's Sioux had been dealt with up near the Great Lakes. The *News* pointed out they'd hung thirty-odd Sioux leaders and recovered *all* the white girls the savage sons of bitches hadn't finished off entire. So it wasn't Eagle Chief, as the Indians were commencing to call John Chivington, who nursed a private grudge against Mr. Lo.

I got to vote that November for the very first time. In spite of rumors to the contrary, Chivington's name never appeared on the ticket of either party that fall, whether his enemies were right or wrong about his political ambitions. I knew McClellan would mess up as President as dithersome as he'd messed up as a general at Antietam. So I voted for Abe Lincoln and, since he'd asked for Andrew Johnson as his running mate, I voted for that old windbag, too.

A nester and his teenage son, riding in to Denver about the same time, got jumped and scalped out on the open prairie. I wasn't there, but they say both bodies had been pin-cushioned with blue-striped and crow feather-vaned Cheyenne arrows.

I was still surprised, next muster day, to find myself riding south, out on point, without even having had a chance to go home and tell Martha we were off to fight us some Indians.

Colonel Chivington had taken personal command of six hundred picked men, chosen more by their records than their designated units from the two active regiments. Most seemed to be from the newer Third Colorado. Poor Lieutenant Colonel George L. Shoup, the Third's nominal CO, got to tag along as second-in-command, leastways.

But Colonel Chivington didn't tell Shoup or anyone else where on earth we were headed until we were well out of Denver. Out on point with Jim Beckwourth I was able to make an educated guess, even before Jim said we seemed to be bee-lining south-south-east for Fort Lyon.

When you mention November in connection with the High Plains of Colorado Territory, you've just mentioned bitter weather. An early snow had already come and gone, so the rolling prairie all around was a big old brown-and-white pinto hide under a sullen gray sky. Colonel Chivington set the same killing pace we older hands recalled from that expedition to save Santa Fe for the Union. Some of the greener members of the Bloodless Third opined the old fart had to be *loco en la cabeza* if he thought we could keep this up much further.

But we did keep it up, riding column-of-fours ahint the fluttering guidons, with the chuck wagons and a brace of field guns and their caissons of cannister and bomb shells. The colonel's chosen line of march avoided any settled parts. We was making thirty or forty miles a day, depending on how often the heavy field guns bogged. The colonel set an example and won over some of the new recruits by sharing their literally rotten rations. The War Department was supposed to issue militia the same ordnance and supplies the regulars got, only they never did. Colonel Chivington had everyone laughing fit to bust when he dug some live maggots out of his half-cooked hash and yelled, "Who says this meat isn't fresh, boys? Look at how it wiggles on my fork? If that's not fresh meat, what is?"

By now we were at least two-thirds of the way and most of us had guessed where we had to be headed. Colonel Chivington called a staff meeting in his tent, about the third campsite out, and told us were on our way to where we'd figured, because the post commander at Fort Lyon said the Indians were getting out of hand again and that he just didn't have the men to bust some heads.

George Shoup whistled softly and said he'd heard young Wynkoop had been letting the sassy redskins just about run the post whilst they called him Tall Chief and buttered him up one side and down the other.

Chivington smiled thinly and explained, "Wynkoop was relieved of his command just before election time. There might or might not have been some connection. There were some complaints, as you just mentioned."

Jim Beckwourth asked who, in that case, was having so much Indian trouble down yonder, Chivington replied, "The new CO would be a Major Anthony. Scott J. Anthony, I believe."

Jim Beckwourth swore and said, "I know him. The Indians call him Red Eye. It's been said Major Anthony don't like *them* all that much, neither."

Chivington shrugged and said, "I understand he's had more experience as an Indian-fighter than young Wynkoop. Agent Colley at the fort backs Anthony. Apparently both the Arapaho and Cheyenne have been openly defying orders."

"What kind of orders?" asked Jim.

The colonel shrugged and said, "Any orders a white officer wants to give an Indian he's responsible for, I suppose. Our job is not to feed Mr. Lo with a spoon, gentlemen. They have an agent assigned to do that. Our job is to make the rascals abide by the rules with this, ah, show of force."

Jim Beckwourth asked what John Smith, the Bents, and other white informants had had to say about Anthony's run-ins with the Indians. Chivington said, "Nothing, so far. Just who's side those squaw-men and their half-breed spawn might be on is up for grabs. But I agree it makes sense to hear what they have to say about the trouble before we charge in blind."

EAGLE CHIEF                                                    107

Jim Beckwourth said, "*Bueno.* I'll scout up Pawnee Joe and that fool nigger who keeps saying he's a Seminole and we can get there a good twenty-four hours ahead of the main column, Lord willing, and we keep our hair."

Chivington shot a thoughtsome glance my way and said, "I want you to ride on ahead with Sergeant Clark here. I'll just keep those breeds back here with me, for now, if you don't mind."

Jim shot me an odd look and didn't say anything for a long time. Then he nodded and softly replied, "You're the boss, Colonel. Seeing you'd trust this white boy afore you'd trust any of us treachersome older scouts with, ah, better suntans."

I said, "Aw, Jim, for Pete's sake . . ."

To which he replied, not looking at me, "Let's go, Goldielocks, we got a long, cold ride ahead of us."

Jim tried to stay sore at me, as he had every right to, but as we rode south together over frost-rimmed buffalo-grass stubble, which reminded me of Martha's swell coconut cake icing, the old darky didn't have it in him. I told him how the colonel had asked me to keep an eye on him and Jim said, "I know. You ain't the only one. I ain't got a drop more Indian blood in me than he does, but ever since I told him they'd named me Medicine Calf that time I wintered over with Leg In Water—"

I cut in to explain, "He's more worried about your pals who *do* have Indian blood, Jim. I can't say I disagree with him in full. Ain't both Roman Nose and Quanah Parker at least as white as, say, the Bent boys or that grown son of Uncle John Smith?"

Jim shrugged and said, "Mebbe. I take anything I hears off *anybody* with a grain of salt. How come Colonel Chivington don't suspicion Red Eye Anthony or Sam Colley, the agent at Fort Lyon?"

I frowned and said, "You told me Scott Anthony's known to be an Indian-hater. What's the story on that agent, Colley? Are you saying he's out to cause trouble for the very Indians he's supposed to be there to help?"

Jim shrugged and replied, "I don't know the man, personal.

Calling an Indian agent a troublemaker is like doubting the
virginity of a whore. Half of 'em don't know what they're
doing and them as do are as anxious to feather their own nests
as they are to help an Indian. The pay is modest, the graft is
immense. If you follow my drift.''

I did, but suggested, ''I'll go along with an Indian agent
cheating his clients if you'll allow it'd be dumb to kill any
geese laying golden eggs, Jim. Why would even a crooked
Indian agent want to see his Indians shot off?''

Jim said he didn't know, and suggested we get on down to
Fort Lyon and find out. So that's what we did.

Fort Lyon, on the north bank of the Arkansas about twenty
miles downstream of the original Bent's fort, was named for
Union Captain Nathaniel Lyon, who got killed heroic at
Wilson's Creek, Missouri, the first year of the war. It was
located on the ruins of Bent's New Fort, built by William Bent
just afore the war, that had been swept away by a flood as
bodacious as the one up Denver way.

As rebuilt by the army engineers, Fort Lyon was more a
small town with a modest sod wall around it than a riverside
castle. As Jim and me rode in, I noticed big burnt circles in the
grass stubble outside the gate. Jim said that was funny, because
as a rule you saw at least a few dozen Indian lodges pitched
outside the walls of any such outpost. It was generally held
more practical to suffer a few nubile squaws for the unmarried
enlisted men than it was to have them pestering the white gals
inside the walls.

The main gate was left open during daylight hours to save
having to open and shut it all day. Aside from travelers asking
for shelter in such trying times, the only post office, telegraph
office, and other places whites might have lawsome business
lay inside the walls, facing the big open parade in the center.
There was a soldier lounging in the gateway, half-asleep. He
didn't see fit to pester us, so we had no call to pester him. We
reined in in front of the trading post and dismounted, to tether
our ponies and sashay in for some beer and gossip.

The plump young breed gal ahint the counter allowed the
laws forbidding the sale of firewater didn't apply to Jim, de-

spite his fringed buckskins. So we had our beers needled a mite
with trade likker, the strong stuff they make not to sell to
Indians.

When Jim asked the gal how come no lodges seemed to be
pitched out front she glanced about as if to make sure this was
a private conversation and confided, "Red Eye chased them
away. Most of the Cheyenne had already gone into winter camp
with Motavato. There were some Arapaho out there when Tall
Chief went away and Red Eye came to take over. He told the
Arapaho they were too close to the fort. When they argued with
him, he had his soldiers fire a volley into their lodges."

Jim and I exchanged thoughtsome glances. Jim asked, "*Into*
the lodges? Not *over* them?"

She shook her head firmly and said, "The soldiers thought
it was funny. They laughed as they picked out medicine signs
on the lodge covers for targets. No Arapaho were killed. A
few, they say, were wounded, but not too badly to run away.
Most of them were from Left Hand's band. Jack Smith, the son
of Gray Blanket, told us they'd gone to join Motavato in the
big bend of Sand Creek."

Jim whistled and said, "Damn, that puts Black Kettle and
Left Hand, combined, smack on the limits of this post's juris-
diction. I wonder why the regulars, here, sent all the way up to
Denver for us. If they cross Sand Creek they'll be in dutch with
Colonel Greenwood at Fort Larned, down the river into Kan-
sas."

I didn't find it as mysterious. I said, "This Anthony jasper
sent for the militia to help him because he ain't so sure the
regular army would *want* to."

Jim whistled and said, "You're right. I got to scout up old
John Smith or one of the Bents, pronto."

The girl had been listening. She said, "Neither Gray Blanket nor any of the Bents are here, now. Some say they went to
trade with my mother's people. Others say Red Eye sent them
all away, for some reason."

Jim Beckwourth asked me to sort of hold the fort for the
colonel whilst he scouted up someone who could tell us what

in thunder might be going on. I didn't have the rank to pester field-grade officers or even Indian agents, so I reported in to the orderly room and the regimental sergeant major, a decent enough cuss for a regular, said it was jake with him if I wanted to mess and bunk with the outfit till my own showed up, as long as I behaved myself.

When a green lance corporal showed me where I could stable my pony and spread my own bedding, I took the opportunity to ask him about the Indian trouble they'd been having. He shrugged and told me the only trouble he'd been having was getting laid, now that a certain Arapaho gal had been hauled off weepy-eyed. He said he'd heard most of the Arapaho had lit out to the south under Little Raven and to hell with any deal they'd made with Doc Evans. We'd later hear *that* band had fallen in with the Kiowa in time for that swell Buffalo War on the Staked Plains we all recall so fondly. Left Hand and his own Arapaho had fallen in with Black Kettle, forty miles off to the northeast. The lance corporal said Major Anthony found that ominous. He wasn't sure whether the major thought the combined Indian bands were too close or too far. He and that trading post gal agreed a whole heap of Indians had gone into winter camp in the big bend of Sand Creek, up a piece from where Rush Creek forks into it so's they can both spill into the Arkansas as one, weather permitting.

I et my noon dinner in the enlisted mess. It wasn't bad as long as you liked galvanized pork, desecrated potatoes, and coffee bitter enough to cure the ague. The military always seems to buy the best-quality grub and then treat it just awful.

Seeing they weren't short of grub, bad as it might be prepared, I asked the regulars eating next to me if they'd had to give any of this swell swill to the Indians, so far. The notion seemed to strike them mighty odd. A freckle-faced private said he'd been on the detail when Major Anthony had offered some Indians grub in exchange for their firearms. He continued, "They didn't get much. We knew they was holding out when all they produced was one pistol, three old flintlock rifles, and some fool bows and arrows."

Another regular said, "They was Arapaho, sucking around

the post for handouts. The sneaky Cheyenne are holed up further out, just itching for the chance to hit us.''

The one with freckles repressed a shudder and said, ''I hear tell that when Cheyenne scalp you they peel your whole fool head and sometimes they take along your right arm as well.''

I didn't argue. What he'd heard was the simple truth. But anyone could see they were green as well as proddy. That late in the war all the privates left were raw recruits or, if they were old enough to shave regular, worthless soldiers.

After I'd et, the day sort of dragged on. Jim had said the Bents were raising beef and produce further down the river when they weren't trading with the Indians. I figured he'd gone to jaw with Little White Man, the daddy Bent. I'd been at Camp Weld long enough to know some officious shavetail would ask me to paint him white if he saw me doing nothing more useful. So I got out my pony and rid out a piece to see what could be keeping the rest of the outfit.

I met up with 'em less'n four miles out of the fort. Colonel Chivington was a forced-marching fool when it come to getting across country. As I reined in, I told him all Jim and me had found out, so far. He didn't seem too happy to hear Jim had ridden for the Bent's ranch. He waved a shavetail from the Third over to snap, ''Lieutenant, I want you to pick two dozen good men and get on over to the ranch of William Bent. You'll find it less than five miles down the river. If you find Jim Beckwourth there, tell him he's to rejoin me at the fort, on the double. Then I want you to secure the ranch and make sure not a living soul rides out until further notice. Are there any questions?''

The shavetail frowned and said, ''Yessir. Are your orders to arrest anyone and, if so, may I ask on what charge?''

Chivington replied, ''You're not to place anyone under formal arrest as long as they cooperate. So you'll need no charge, Lieutenant. Old Bent has a swarm of half-breed kids and at least one French Canadian son-in-law who spends more time with Mr. Lo than I want anyone to spend until I get a better handle on this situation. So what are you waiting for, a kiss goodbye?''

The shavetail got cracking as the colonel waved the column on. As we rode he questioned me about conditions at the fort ahead. I told him the little I knew. When he heard Uncle John Smith had gone off some place in this weather and that Jim was searching for any of the Bent boys left, Colonel Chivington twisted in his saddle to call Short-Colonel Shoup closer. As his second-in-command fell in Chivington said, "We'll be pitching our own tents around the walls of the fort in any case, George. Young Clark, here, tells me they've been letting civilians, some of them half-Indian, ride in or out at will. Pending contrary orders from the post commander, I want that to cease and desist. Tell your sergeant-of-the-guard he's to let anyone with legitimate business in but nobody *out* without a pass signed by me or the Post OD. Any questions?"

Shoup nodded and said, "I understand the stagecoaches running betwixt Missouri and Santa Fe lay over there after dark. Do we have the authority to interfere with cross-country travel and the U.S. Mail?"

Chivington thought, shrugged, and decided, "We could be saving some scalps as well as some love letters. Major Anthony has the final authority, of course, but unless the regulars countermand me, do as I say. We're not going to be holding anyone against their will all that long. Meanwhile, the less Mr. Lo knows about our movements the better!"

Shoup said he'd see to it that the colonel's orders were carried out. As we rode on, Chivington questioned me further. I had to allow I'd only taken a quick peek around Fort Lyon, having neither the social nor the military rank to invite myself into anyone's quarters for tea.

Colonel Chivington did. A regular officer on a prancing thoroughbred came out to greet us and tell the colonel they were expecting him at their officers' club with plenty of refreshments. Chivington said he didn't drink but that he sure wanted to get together with Anthony and plot some disciplinary action.

I got to ride with them as far as the officers' club, facing the parade. Major Scott J. Anthony, his junior officers, and some officious-looking civilians were waiting for us, or at least for the colonel, on the front veranda. I knew right off which one was Red Eye. Aside from the gold oak leaves on the shoulders of his dress blues, the little squinty runt had some awful eye infection as made 'em all red-rimmed and runny. I later heard it was scurvy but, hell, half the men in the regular army had scurvy and none of 'em looked *that* red-eyed.

Be that as it may, the major seemed otherwise healthy as he greeted the colonel and invited him inside to talk about killing Indians.

I dismounted as well, and would have tagged along had not a young squirt with spanking new gold bars asked where I thought I was going with them dusty sergeant stripes. So I figured I'd go somewheres else instead.

I put my pony away and traipsed out the gate to scout up less frosty company. The Colorado Volunteers were already starting to pitch their pyramid tents. Six hundred men were pitching a hundred and fifty-odd tents—I can see how some said, later, that Colonel Chivington had surrounded Fort Lyon and taken it over like some sort of big old pirate. But, for the record, Fort Lyon was a regular army post, and militia take over toad squat from the regular army at their own peril, even when they're *Confederate* militia.

I spied Jim Beckwourth riding into the far side of our new tent city and hailed him. He joined me, dismounted, and as the two of us walked over to the gate to put Jim's own pony in the stable he told me, "Bill Bent says young Major Anthony is either crazy-mean or spooked worse'n a schoolmarm in a mouse-infested crapper. There ain't no Indians within miles. Anthony's reversed all Wynkoop's policies. So there's nothing to keep Indian-One anywheres near the ugly red-eyed runt."

I told him some of the regulars seemed as spooked by not seeing any lodges out here now, as they might have been by, say, a bevy of drunken squaws.

Jim said, "Most of 'em have scattered far and wide into winter camps. Bill Bent says Black Kettle, White Antelope, and Left Hand of the Arapaho have joined forces against the starving months up in the big bend of Sand Creek. Bill says he'd know if they were plotting anything or even holding them missing white gals. His two younger boys, George and Charlie, are with 'em now. George Bent's been courting Black Kettle's niece, Magpie. Can't say I blame him. She's a right pretty little thing. Their brother-in-law, Guerrier, may be up yonder as well. Bill Bent sent him out with some trade goods to see if they have any prime fall robes to sell.''

I told him what the colonel had said about civilians that might gossip about troop movements. Jim looked disgusted and said, ''Well, he don't have to worry about old Bill Bent. Some soldiers were riding in to place him under house arrest as I was leaving. They was going to hold *me*, too, till one of the older hands recognized this old black face of mine. The only one as might tip the Indians off would be Uncle John Smith. One of Bill Bent's cowhands told me Gray Blanket and his oldest boy, Jack, left the fort just yesterday after some discussion with young Major Anthony. The hand couldn't say whether it had been friendly or otherwise.''

I grimaced and allowed that, having seen both gents in the flesh, I doubted they could ever be good pals. Jim frowned and mused, half to himself, ''We'd best warn the colonel that Gray Blanket could have heard Anthony sent for help. They told me at the Bent spread that the old man and his boy were only after buffalo robes, the same as anyone else trading with Indians after the fall hunt. But you never know.''

I said, ''Correct me if I'm wrong. But ain't it unusual for Indians to have a heap of robes on hand right after the army's busted up a hunt?''

Jim said, ''You ain't wrong. I just *said* we'd best warn the colonel.''

The Colorado Volunteers spent the next twenty-odd hours doing nothing much and resting up from the forced march down from Denver. Me and the other scouts got to range out from the fort a piece lest howling savages descend on well over eight hundred men, armed with everything from skinning knives to twelve-pounder field guns. So I only managed to keep track of what was going on in and about Fort Lyon in bits and pieces as I came back in to warm up betwixt patrols. Patrolling on the High Plains of Colorado in November calls for warming up indeed. And December was approaching, whilst the infernal big shots made up their infernal minds in the warmth of the infernal officer's club.

Being a humble militia staff sergeant, I had to guess at some of the details I'd later have to swear to at a congressional hearing. But everyone seems agreed that Major Anthony found all them Indians gathered in the sort of no-man's-land betwixt his jurisdiction and that of Fort Larned, down the Arkansas, mighty ominous. I can't say how ominous Colonel Chivington might have found it if the Indian agent, Sam Colley, hadn't backed the post commander up and then some. Colley said the Indians had gobbled up rations meant to see them through the winter in less'n two weeks, and then demanded the army issue more. Nobody but Jim Beckwourth seemed to notice the contrary way Major Anthony's orders to his charges read. On the one hand he'd told 'em they weren't about to get any army rations unless they turned in all their hunting rifles. On the other hand, he opined they were a nation of lazy slobs if they expected the army to feed 'em when all they had to do was hunt their own damned food as they'd always done.

As we were enjoying some suds near the potbelly in the trading post, Jim told me both the breeds and pure whites trading with the Indians thought Agent Colley had been holding back on government rations. Jim said, "Bill Bent says the squaws have been asking him for salt pork and corn grits. They never *trade* for such staples as a rule. They're supposed to get their papoose fodder off the Great White Father and trade for luxury goods like red ribbons and licorice whips. Bent says he never sold half the simple groceries he does now afore Colley took over here."

I asked if he'd told the colonel as much. Jim nodded and said, "He said it stands to reason all these extra Indians eat more than the B.I.A. allotted Colley to issue till recent. Wynkoop was a known Indian-lover and he never complained about Colley whilst he was in command."

I said that made sense to me and asked Jim what was really

eating him, since anyone could see something was. The wise old maroon made a wry face and declared, "I fears we're being used. Red Eye could have wired his own headquarters and had other regulars here sooner, if he had a convincing tale to tell. General Curtis hates Indians at least as much as Colonel Chivington could."

I said, "Anthony might admire the colonel's tendency to whip out that terrible swift sword and charge off cliffs. One of the garrison here said something about Anthony having lived in Denver one time. He may have heard about Glorieta Pass."

Jim grimaced and insisted, "General Curtis can act terrible to Indians, too. Another professional scout I know, James Butler Hickock, rode with Curtis at Pea Ridge agin Confederate Cherokee. Scattered 'em like chaff and kilt a rebel general whilst he was at it. They rewarded him with his western command for taking Arkansas away from the South. Does that sound like a man who'd shy at slaughtering any Indians as needed slaughtering?"

I said he sounded like a fighting fool. Jim shook his head sadly and said, "Colonel Chivington's the fighting fool, old son. You was there. You like to brag about charging over cliffs with him. John Chivington is as brave, or as loco, as any fighting man I've ever rid with. But I surely wish he'd *think* a mite more about what he might be *doing* when he whips out that terrible swift sword!"

Before I could answer, that freckle-faced garrison trooper came in to tell us we were wanted over at the officers' club. The colonel wanted us scouts in on it as he finalized his plans. That's what they call it when they're ready to roll the dice— finalizing the plans.

Jim answered direct questions, and I got to say even less that afternoon in the officers' club. Major Anthony and Colonel Chivington had already agreed to finalize the Indians pretty good, when one considers that Jim Beckwourth and Indian Agent Colley both agreed Black Kettle had mayhaps five hundred souls, most of them women and children, in his winter camp along Sand Creek. We'd left Denver with two field guns and six hundred militiamen. Major Anthony had chipped in a hundred cavalry troopers and a battery of four heavier field guns. Old Red Eye said he'd sure like to tag along, but that somebody had to hold the fort. Captain Silas Soule and Lieutenants Cramer and Conner were to come along and command the regulars. Later, all three were going to testify under oath that they'd only come along under protest after Chivington cussed 'em out and threatened to court-martial them.

They may or may not have had their doubts about serving under a sort of wild-looking militia officer, albeit anyone can see they wouldn't have had to unless their regular major ordered 'em to. I don't recall anyone protesting at the time. I do recall that in them days, betwixt, say, the Battle of the Mormon Cow and Wounded Knee, every officer or enlisted man who served anywheres near an Indian got to sport a bitty red-and-blue campaign ribbon. But if he wanted anything *else* on his chest he had to take part in some officious action such as the Wagon Box Fight, the Battle of Beecher Island (where Roman Nose would finally get it), or whatever. I suspicion the boys from Fort Lyon were as ready as the rest of us to pick up a battle bar that cold crisp afternoon.

It was now, let's see, the 28th of November, 1864, and Colonel Chivington gave orders we all enjoy a good hot supper and pack three days' rations in our saddlebags. Then after dark, with nary a soul to be allowed out of Fort Lyon for twenty-four hours, we marched off to meet the foe in a column of fours, our ponies well rested and full of oats. If it hadn't been so dark we'd have made quite a sight, what with the supply wagons and field artillery trailing after more than seven hundred riders.

The rolling prairie was frozen firm, and the dried grass was so frosty it shattered like glass under our steel-shod hooves and rolling wheels. I was way out, riding flank picket, so I didn't hear just what the colonel and Jim Beckwourth were arguing about, if they really were, as some recalled, later. It sure seems strange how so many men who rode with us that night recalled it all so different.

Our point scout, Pawnee Joe, spied window lights ahead. I was one of the riders as circled and secured the outlying cattle

spread. It belonged to Bob Bent, Little White Man's eldest
son, who was naturally half-Cheyenne but inclined to live
more white than his younger kin. I think his momma was Owl
Woman, Bill Bent's first and most civilized squaw.

At any rate, old Bob seemed sort of uneasy as he stood there
in his front parlor, half-dressed, with his Indian wife and kids
peeking out at us wide-eyed from the back. As Jim Beckwourth led the colonel in and introduced him to Bob Bent, the
colonel said, "You'd best dress warmly. We want you to show
us the way to Black Kettle's winter camp."

Bob Bent looked thundergasted and protested he wasn't any
damned army scout, and that even if he had been, Colonel
Chivington was talking mighty wild. Bent said, "My two kid
brothers are over yonder with Motavato, along with Ed Guerrier and Uncle John Smith. Young Jack Smith, too. Do you
really think that many whites would be visiting a hostile band,
Colonel?"

Chivington chuckled and replied, "With all due respect to
your no-doubt sainted mothers, neither you Bent brothers nor
the Smith boy are what I'd define as a white man, and I can't
help having certain reservations about a man who calls himself
John Smith while cohabitating with another race. Be that as it
may, get dressed and saddle up a good mount, Robert Bent. If
your baby brothers are camping among friendly Arapaho and
Cheyenne none of you have anything to worry about. Friendly
or not, Black Kettle has gathered too many followers too far
from the army post and Indian agency he was assigned to. I
mean to break up that mob and move everyone back to Fort
Lyon."

Bob Bent said, "I ain't sure they'll want to go, Colonel. It's
bitter cold, and there's neither the food nor the shelter anywhere else in these parts."

Chivington said, "It won't be for them to say. Get dressed
more warmly or come along in your shirt-sleeves. Either way,
you're coming."

So Bob Bent came with us, wrapped in a sheepskin coat,
with his hat tied down over his ears with a wool muffler. I had
the muffler Martha's mother had knit for me wrapped around

my own fool head that bitter night, and I sure blessed the sweet old lady for being so thoughtful as we rode on, and on, for forty damned frozen miles.

We crossed Rush Creek, or at least we crossed ice froze fast to the very bottom. Jim whistled me into the head of the column a few miles further on. Colonel Chivington said, "Whether they know we're coming or not, they're sure to escape on their ponies unless we secure their remuda, first. Bent says they have most of their ponies amid second-growth cottonwoods, downstream from the main camp. I want you to lead your own patrol in that way, Clark, and see how many mounts you can capture or scatter before the fun and games begin."

I said I'd try if he'd keep it in mind I was a scout and not a fancy squad leader. Bob Bent had been listening, half-froze, in his own saddle. He protested, "This is loco, Colonel! Let me ride in ahead and see if I can't get the three sagamores to surrender sedate! You're sure to have a firefight if you send this kid in after their ponies, first!"

Chivington shrugged and said, "I'm sending him in to cut off any escape, anyway. Are there any questions, Clark?"

I answered, "Yessir. What are my boys and me supposed to do about any Indians we find in the company of said ponies?"

Chivington said, bleakly, "Kill them, if you have to. *They* don't take grown men prisoners, unless they mean to have a little fun with them. We don't torture prisoners, so feel free to do whatever you have to."

Bent almost wailed, "You crazy butcher! Most of the folk you're about to jump are women and children!"

Chivington seemed to ignore him, but said to me, and I recall his exact words, "I don't tell you to kill all ages and sex, but look back on where white fathers, mothers, and children have been murdered and mutilated as you use your own judgment, as the circumstances may warrant."

Yeah, I know. It could be taken either way, and was, within the next few hours. Suffice it to say, them was his exact orders as to taking or not taking prisoners.

I selected eight Denver boys I knew to be sensible and stuck with the head of the column till the sky ahead commenced to pearl lighter and Jim said, "Sand Creek ain't more'n a couple of furlongs ahead, now. I know you can't see nothing. That's what makes it a good winter camp. The flat wide creekbed's treetop-deep of the wolf winds blowing mean across the general grade of all this frosty buffalo grass."

Jim turned to me and added in a softer tone, "You'll want to get going if you're going, Ross. Take your boys toward that bitty red star hanging low to the southeast. Dismount near some soap weeds you'll find on a rise too close for comfort and then take your boys in the rest of the way afoot. You may find the ponies unguarded at this ungodly hour. If anyone is keeping an eye on 'em don't fool with 'em. You'll be tangling with a *hotamitano*, or dog soldier, and you don't want to fool around with *them* boys!"

Bob Bent protested, "You damned bloodthirsty nigger! You're as much as telling this kid to commit cold-blooded murder!"

Jim morosely replied, "I know what I'm telling him to do, Bob. They call me Medicine Calf, and you're more Tsitsissah than I am. So do we really have to bullshit one another as to how this game is played?"

We almost pulled it off peaceable. Jim must have really had the country down this way mapped good in his head. For we come upon a clump of soap weed, or what the Mexicans call yucca, right where he said we would. I reined in my patrol and told 'em to dismount silent. For whilst I still couldn't see a lodge pole, I could smell a big camp, even this far out.

We left one old boy holding the ponies whilst I led the other seven in, sort of crouched. It ain't snobbish to say you can smell an Indian camp and recognize it as such from some distance. You can smell a white settlement or even a white homestead if you've been breathing purer country air a spell. Think of autumn leaves, dried corn stalks, a little bacon grease, and a dash of horse and that's close enough to what an Indian camp smells like on a crisp November dawn.

Sand Creek was way bigger and hence deeper than Cherry Creek up Denver way. I led my patrol along the west rim until the stars near the eastern horizon across the way were commencing to vanish. Lem Bancroft kept saying the damned old sun was going to catch us in the open and get us all kilt and scalpt, or worse. Then I heard a pony nicker in the blurry blackness of the bare cottonwoods down yonder. We unslung our carbines and slid down the steep bank on our rumps, with long guns across our guts at port arms. I was packing a six-gun on each hip, of course. Scouts seldom had anybody covering for 'em as they had to reload.

By the time we'd worked our way through the tanglewood to the Indian ponies, it was almost light enough to make out colors. Horse Indians liked to winter their mounts amongst cottonwoods, because even when they've dropped their leaves a pony can browse on cottonwood twigs if it's really hungry.

We were in luck. The considerable remuda was pent inside a rope corral. I told the boys to see if they could cut the ropes on the south side and sort of drift the stock off discreet whilst I covered for 'em betwixt the corral and the camp just up the creek bed.

It started out all right. I told you I'd picked boys I knew to have some sense, and it's easy enough to drift a pony silent if you don't try to move either one of you too sudden. But just as I figured we'd pulled her off and it was safe for me to crawfish back through the trees as well, all hell busted loose.

I don't know who fired first, or how come. I only know that all of a sudden there come this popcorn crackle of small-arms fire underscored by the deep, tinny coughs of cannon clearing their throats.

I'd just had time to notice that when this rascal wearing a red flannel shirt and no pants come down the draw at me waving a wicked stone-tipped war quirt and yelling at me fit to bust. I've yet to decide whether he was a dog soldier patrolling the camp for thieves like me or just an early riser. Either way, I shot him flat.

Then another come at me as I was reloading my Sharps. He had this feathered lance fashioned from a twisty sapling *I'd* have never picked, and I saw he was likely to stick me with it if I let him. So I dropped my Sharps and went for the cross-draw Colt on my left hip. Then a round of cannister saved me the trouble, and almost took me with the crooked-lancer as it landed just the other side of him.

I ducked in time for all the iron balls and most of the torn-up Indian to fly over me, harmless, as I yelled, "Not *me*, you stupid sons of bitches!" as more cannister come in to stir up heaps of dust, with bomb shells landing, even louder, to fill the whole area with billowing white gun smoke!

I half rose behind a stout cottonwood trunk to see if I could get my bearings. Way off in the smoke I spied the Stars and Stripes waving in the morning breeze. So I headed for it. How was I supposed to know it was that big old garrison flag Black Kettle had pitched above his big lodge in the center of the infernal camp?

I had to pass other lodges first. As I approached one, a bombshell landed on the far side. By the orange light flashing through the oiled hide, I had a sudden glimpse of the lodge poles and the outline of a willowsome figure inside. Then I was lying flat on my back with the wrecked lodge and the squaw who'd been inside it on top of me. I shoved all the splinted wood and mangled squaw off me so's I could move.

I'd lost my Sharps, somewhere, by now. I'd lost my hat and that muffler Martha's mother had knit for me, too, damn it. I forged on toward that fool flag, six-gun in hand. A bitty, bare-ass baby girl come tottering toward me through the smoke, bawling fit to bust. I called out to the Indian tyke but, before she could decide one way or the other, someone else nailed her, either deliberate or accidental. A baby girl sure goes flying, when she's hit in the head with a rifle ball. I was crying by this time. Likely on account of all the smoke in my fool eyes. It was tough to make head or tails out of what was going on. Another Indian woman came staggering through the swirling smoke at me, her hands out in front of her as if she was playing blind-man's buff, only that wasn't it. Her eyes were gone, and you could see white bone and ghastly grinning teeth through the red ruin of her shot-off face. So I killed her.

You would have, too, if you'd been there and had an ounce of mercy in you.

I heard someone singing. I had one of the Bents write the words down for me, later. It was crazy to hear such a wistful chant coming my way amid all them shots and bloody screamings. It was old White Antelope. He was standing near the doorway of his lodge, with his blanket draped around his otherwise bare body like a Roman toga as he chanted,

> Hear me,
>> Nothing lives forever,
>>> Nothing lives long,
>>>> Nothing but the earth, the mountains,
>>>>> And the sky lives forever.

He sang it in his own lingo, of course, and whether it had any more words or not another rifle ball thunked into the old man to finish him and his death song, as if to prove how right it had been.

I moved on toward the Stars and Stripes. I could see it was waving above Black Kettle's central lodge, now. They'd run up a big white flag beside it and a heap of Indians, mostly women and children, were huddled there bawling with fright. Some of the Indian women had their skirts up to expose their privates, to show what they were. A couple were already down. As bullets thunked into such tempting targets, those as could lit out, screaming like hell whether they'd been hit or not. I saw more than one *had* been hit, bad. I called out, "Hold your damned fire! Can't you see they're just women?" and then somebody sent a rifle ball right by *my* left ear so I run off as well. I run almost smack into an Indian coming the other way, an Arapaho if the green ribbons in his hair meant anything. I had to shoot him, and then I run around this shot-up lodge only to almost trip over another old boy who was tougher to figure. He was already down with a couple of rounds in him. He was dressed half-Indian and had features to match. But when he wailed, "Don't shoot! I'm white! Halfways white, leastways!" I hauled him off into some tanglewood, telling him who *I* was

and asking him if he knew what was going on, since I was
mighty confused.

He said, "I'm Charlie Bent. I come up here with my brother,
George, and now I've been shot, twice, and I still don't know
why!"

I said, "Your older brother Bob is with us. Now I'm fixing
to get rid of your fool beaded hat band and this dumb feather
and, with luck, we'll get you out of this alive. Just remember
that we're all in this together against the savage redskins,
Charlie."

He groaned, "Present company excused, I'd argue some on
who's the *savages* around here! Who in the hell told you to
attack this camp, Sarge? All three sagamores along this old
creek are friendlies!"

I said, "Not White Antelope. I just seen him die. What
about Black Kettle and that Arapaho chief they told us to watch
out for?"

Charlie Bent looked thundergasted and said, "Left Hand
ain't no hostile. He joined Motavato here, lest they confuse
him and his band with wilder Arapaho to the south of the
Arkansas. Last I seen of old Motavato, or Black Kettle, as you
call him, he was packing his wife piggyback up the draw.
She'd been hit. Bad, judging from all the blood running down
the old man's leggings. I don't know where Left Hand is now.
If he lives you're fixing to have one pissed-off Arapaho on your
hands in the future! You say you can get me to my big brother
Bob?"

By now the artillery fire had petered out. I said, "I can try.
The outfit will be moving in personal to mop up, now. So keep
your hat brim down and let me do the talking."

Then I hauled him to his feet, got one of his arms draped
over my shoulder, and grabbed his belt on the far side with my
left hand so's I could hold a six-gun in my right as we stag-
gered off together like a pair of drunks trying to get home in the
cold gray dawn.

It was a way more confusing battlefield than that chaparral
flat down New Mexico way. Winter-bare trees and Indian
lodges in various states of disrepair loomed ghostly in the haze

of dust and gunsmoke. By now the sun was up a mite, but its
rays weren't making it down into the deep draw, yet. I told
young Bent we were trying to make it to the wagons up the far
side, and that it'd help if he'd try a mite harder.

We almost tripped over a downed Indian. Charlie sobbed,
"Aw, shit, that's old Left Hand! Is he dead?"

I said, "If he ain't he's sure giving a good imitation!" We
dragged on until we came upon two snot-nosed Indian kids
trying to haul the boots off a dead trooper. Bent yelled at 'em
in Tsitsissah and they run off, laughing, afore I could get off
more than one shot. The next trooper we come upon was
raping a thirteen- or fourteen-year-old squaw atop the ruins of
a knocked-down lodge. He glanced up, grinning like a shit-
eating dog, and this time my aim was better.

Charlie said, "I didn't see that, and you're all right, Sarge."

Then, looming like a bear in the mist ahead, I spied Colonel
Chivington atop a pile of debris, still feeling bulletproof as he
waved his saber about, bellowing orders. As he spied us he
called out, "I told you to secure those horses, Clark! What
have you got there?"

I called back, "We captured their horses. Half of 'em, leastways, and I'd like to get this wounded man up to the wagons,
with your permission, sir."

Chivington snapped, "Carry on!" then turned his attention
to yet another poor mortal as old John Smith came tottering
toward him from another direction, gibbering with fear and
bleeding down one side of his face, Colonel Chivington
slapped one of his boots with the flat of his sword to bellow,
"To me, old man, if you value your life! You ought to be
ashamed of yourself!"

Whether he was or wasn't, Gray Blanket ran over and threw
himself down at Chivington's feet like a redbone hound who'd
tangled with a razorback and never wanted to do *that* again. I
hauled ass with the wounded breed before the colonel or one of
the other officers I could see now thought to ask more fool
questions.

It wasn't easy but I got Charlie Bent up the far bank, and as
luck would have it we run into Jim Beckwourth between a field

artillery battery and the wagon park. Jim grabbed young Bent on the other side and said, "Nice going, Ross. We'll hide him in a wagon I just stuffed with a wounded officer till his big brother can get him out of here!"

As we got him under cover Jim told Charlie about his brother Bob being around here somewheres. Charlie asked about his brother George. Jim said, "Ain't seen him, so far. He's likely with Magpie, dead or alive. I got Jack Smith hid up ahead, though. He ain't hurt, but he'd sure better keep under cover. He looks way more Indian than any of you Bent boys, and he's dressed mighty fringy as well!"

By this time we'd made it to the ambulance, where one of our officers lay doped to the gills with opium pills. In them days the regular Union Army was just starting to get a medical service. Miss Clara Barton hadn't made her way west of the Mississippi, yet, and so things were sort of informal as we loaded Charlie in and fed *him* some opium. Musicians of the regimental bands served as litter-bearers in battle, and the civilian surgeons, contracted like civilian scouts, took care of the wounded back near headquarters. Colonel Chivington hadn't brung along a band. Jim told me I'd best go keep the colonel happy whilst he scouted up Bob Bent and got both of 'em the hell outten here. So that's what I done.

By the time I rejoined the colonel and the others down in the creek bed, most of the Indian village had been overrun, but the battle was far from over. Black Kettle had picked Sand Creek to winter in because it was wooded, thick, for many a mile, with cottonwood, willow, alder, choke cherry, and such, down to winter-kilt cattails and bullrushes sticking up through the ice of the braided stream down the center of the wide draw.

As well as anyone's ever been able to tally up, Chivington hit four to six hundred Indians with seven hundred men. Most of the Indians were women and children, as the Indians never get tired of saying. About a hundred of 'em were full-fledged pinasees, mostly dog soldiers or crooked-lancers, and they were good. After the first panic they fell back into the tanglewood and dug in, literal. For by this time Mr. Lo had learned to dig fox holes and even trenches, the same as us. We hit 'em at dawn. We did not butcher 'em in their beds. They fought us up and down that wooded draw *all day* and most of 'em got away when the sun went down again at last. Sand Creek was a bitter, hotly contested fight, with the odds on the side of the whites as far as numbers went and the most experienced Cheyenne or Arapaho fighting men making up for the way they were outnumbered by their own superior skills.

I'll admit right off that a heap of our own proved to be rotten shots if not downright cowards, and that all too many of the boys had kept warm during that long night ride with the help of hard liquor. But despite lack of discipline and more savagery than courage on the part of some, there were enough real fighting men in Chivington's command to slowly push the Indians back, and back, up a long strip of mighty thick woods. Here and yonder along the line the Indians would counter and take back a patch of tanglewood. Neither side treated any wounded they captured with Christian charity. I saw men, women and, yes, children, cut up so bad that day that I couldn't buy a human being treating an animal like that in a slaughterhouse.

By the time Jim rejoined me, I'd given up any notion of scouting ahead. We fought shoulder to shoulder with the other Colorado Volunteers and the handful of regulars. It would have been worse than suicide to forge out ahead to locate the enemy positions. It would have been downright *painful*, and there was no mystery about who was in them trees ahead. From time to time a trade rifle would squib and some old boy would lose his hat, if not the top of his head.

It seems that Jim and me fought zealous as anyone else that day, despite the doubts that were commencing to assail us. That's a funny thing about warfare. When you find yourself in a firefight you can't lose if you want to go on living. That's how come conscription works, and how the Turks got captured Christian boys to fight their own kind over in the Holy Land. You can hate your own leaders—a heap of soldiers always have. But whilst loving your enemy works in the Good Book, in practice it can get you killed, and you sure don't want to be killed by Arapaho or Cheyenne. So, like I said, we fought long, hard, and dirty.

By two or three in the afternoon, the wagons and artillery had been moved down to the ruins of Black Kettle's village to get 'em out of the wolf wind and lob shells up the draw into the Indian-haunted trees. I et a cold meal, trying not to notice the torn-up bodies all around. Our own got picked up pronto and covered with tarps, unless the Indians had 'em. But some of the first-kilt Indians still lay in plain sight, and the only thing to be said for a human hit by cannister in November is that they take a mite longer to really stink. It's funny how black blood dries, and how dead limbs slowly twist like burning match stems, though.

Some of the boys took scalps. A regular officer, who'd later say he only served that day under protest, helped himself to White Antelope's privates. Lord knows why. Some say he had the old man's scrotum tanned to use as a tobacco pouch. Would you smoke tobacco outten such a container?

By firelight, after sundown had ended the shooting and allowed the Indians to slip away at last, I was listening as they tallied up the score on paper. After all that fuss, about a hundred-odd women and children had been killed. We'd only nailed twenty-eight of their grown men, mostly in the first confusion. They'd killed nine of us, or at least nine of us had been kilt, including that one rapist, and we had forty-odd wounded on our hands, including prisoners. It ain't true that Colonel Chivington ordered prisoners kilt. We just didn't get to *take* more than a handful, less than a dozen, including Gray Blanket's Cheyenne wife and breed son, Jack Smith, the squaw of another white man at Fort Lyon, and three little kids she said were hers. They might have been. She might have been trying to protect 'em. Nobody messed with any captured women or children but, later, some hero shot Jack Smith without permission and never owned up to it.

Bob Bent was allowed to take his wounded kid brother, Charlie, back to his home spread. The other breed brother, George, was still off with the Indians, somewhere.

More than one on our side had seen Left Hand, the Arapaho chief, go down full of lead. But his body was nowhere to be found and, as Charlie Bent had warned, we now had a mighty pissed-off Arapaho to deal with. Custer would meet Arapaho as well as Cheyenne at Little Big Horn in '76, fighting along-side their Lakota allies.

Black Kettle had gotten away with his wounded wife, as well. So after all that fuss Colonel Chivington had in fact nailed one sagamore outten three and everyone agrees White Antelope had been most harmless of the three. All the other Indians, at least four-fifths of 'em, had gotten away clean. That looked so dumb the officers agreed they'd best amend the score to read five hundred Indians kilt and six hundred ponies captured.

It ain't just a *sin* to tell a lie. Colonel Chivington's brag was about to get him in a whole lot of *trouble*!

The first public reaction to the "Battle Of Sand Creek," as it was first called, was about as Chivington expected. "BULLY FOR OUR COLORADO BOYS!" chortled the first newspaper head-lines as the colonel led his volunteers back to Denver in tri-umph. The *News* decided that, "Among the brilliant feats of Indian Warfare, the recent campaign of our Colorado Volun-teers will stand in History with few if any rivals and none shall exceed it in final results."

Since Kit Carson had meanwhile rounded up the whole Na-vaho nation and marched 'em over to Fort Sumner to plant peach trees, a few reporters naturally wanted to know how come the colonel had taken so few if any prisoners. The colo-nel, or some other damned fool writing press releases for the Hundred Dazers, replied for the record, "It may, perhaps, be unnecessary to explain why we saw no reason to take prison-ers."

Jim Beckwourth and me weren't there to savor the triumph of the now Bloody Third. We were out on the infernal frozen prairie, scouting for infuriated Indians. I was tagging along because Jim had asked me. Jim was hunting high and low for his blood brother, Leg In Water, because, speaking both En-glish and Tsitsissah, he was worried sick after comparing notes with both kinds of folk down around Fort Lyon. The two of us had already agreed Sand Creek had been a mistake. The ques-

130

tion left was how *big* a mistake and what could be said or done
to *salvage* the situation.

Old John Smith and his Indian wife, still mourning their
dead son, Jack, were ready to swear under oath that they'd
arrived at the Indian camp only two days before us, with the
knowledge and permission of Major Anthony.

It got worse. Gray Blanket was an old squaw-man with a
drinker's nose, and his woman was no doubt a lying savage
with a personal ax to grind. But Major Anthony had not only
given the Smiths permission to trade with the Indians he was so
worried about, he'd provided them with *transportation*, and
the teamster who'd taken them and their trade goods out to
Black Kettle's camp, a Private David Louderback, was willing
to swear to it!

Others with connections to Fort Lyon had been at Sand
Creek with full knowledge and permission of the post commander who'd requested Chivington's help in putting down the
impending attack. The white civilian whose pretty Cheyenne
woman had damned near been killed out there was as willing
and eager as Smith and Louderback to testify against old Red
Eye. If only Colonel Chivington had used his head he'd have
been off the hook, but he didn't. Even as Jim and me were
tracking down some sensible Indians to get their side of it, the
colonel was making dumb remarks about nits growing up to be
lice and little Indians growing up to be big Indians.

As Jim and I approached White Man's Fork we suddenly
had company. I found the blue-and-red streaks on the diamond-
shaped faces of the riders all about us more ominous than old
Jim. He softly said, "Don't let on you're spooked. They're
dog soldiers, like our own military police. They wear paint all
the time, on duty as camp guards. The blue streaks signify their
nation. The red streaks down their cheeks are mourning, likely
for what just happened. They're supposed to be so pissed that
they're weeping blood, see?"

I saw, indeed, when a black-and-blue striped arrow thunked
into my saddle swells, close as hell to my puckered private
parts. I tried to ignore it, knowing where it would have really

hit if they hadn't had orders to let us ride in alive and well.

We got some more rawhiding from the women, children, and dogs as we rode down into Leg In Water's camp. Luckily, Indian dogs that really bite wind up as stew meat. Grown Indian gals just like to taunt you by hoisting their skirts to show you they're female and still braver than you. Some of the kids aim pretty good with frozen horse apples and blunt-tipped bird arrows, though, and the hell of it is you can't raise an arm to guard your fool face if you don't want 'em all to laugh at you.

We made it to the sagamore's lodge without getting bruised too serious. Leg In Water scowled out, then invited us in, asking Jim sarcastically if we'd come to scalp more women and children. Jim asked his blood brother to gather a council and switched to Tsitsissah to show it was serious. I got to feel a mite left out as I sat in a dark, smoke-filled lodge with a heap of old Indians who looked sore as hell.

After a time a moon-faced squaw served me a dirty look and some mighty nice stew made outten smoked buffalo tongue and bitter root. It ain't all that bitter if you scrape the red skin off afore you boil it, and coffee with white flour instead of cream and sugar in it don't taste as awful as it sounds, neither.

After they'd jawed each other's ears off and everyone knew they had to see us off or put us up for the night, old Leg In Water switched to English, no doubt to make sure *I* followed his drift as well.

He said, "Hear me! We tried to love the Americans, even when they lied to us. At the big council at Fort Laramie they told us all they wanted was permission to cross our hunting grounds in peace to get at the yellow iron in the shining mountains and beyond. We said we did not mind as long as everyone behaved like brothers. Hear me, we said nothing about anyone building cities and fencing in big farms and ranches where we liked to hunt. But even when they did *this* we tried to love them. But your eagle chief was not satisfied with taking our hunting grounds and killing off our buffalo. Now he has started to kill our women and children for no reason, none! Now there can be no peace! Now the bows are strung and the scalping knives are drawn! Hear me! We know the blue coats are as many as the blades of grass. We know your eagle chief has big guns that can blow away ten pinasees with one shot. We are still going to fight until you kill all of us or we kill all of you! We are Tsitsissah! We are not afraid to die! Tell your eagle chief I have a beautiful death song. Tell him I have spoken!''

Jim allowed he surely would and motioned me to follow him out. He didn't have to do that twice. In the cold again Jim swore, took off his hat, and threw it down to stomp it, yelling, ''Oh, that son of a bitch! Oh, that dirty, lying, mother-loving, two-faced specimen of two-faced yaller dog! And to think all this time I only thought he was *crazy*!''

I murmured, ''Jim, we'd best get outten here. I heard what the old cuss said, in there, but—''

''Not him, not the colonel, that shit-licking Scott J. Anthony at Fort Lyon! We've been used, Ross, used as dirty as two-bit whores with the herds in town! But you're right about us getting out of here. We got to get to Denver and shut the colonel up. Come on, I'll explain what I just found out along the way.''

We mounted up and lit out, with Indian kids throwing horse apples after us. When we'd rid far enough to slow down and rest our ponies a mite, Jim filled me in on how low some men will stoop to make a few dishonest pennies. There was never any serious money involved.

Red Eye Anthony hadn't just wanted Indians killed because he didn't like 'em, albeit he hardly could have done them so dirty if he'd liked 'em as much as he admired his pony.

George Bent, still with the Indians, had been given a good education by his somewhat rustic but prosperous white father. So he'd written some letters at Black Kettle's behest and sent 'em off to the B.I.A.

Yep, Black Kettle had complained, *in writing*, that Indian Agent Colley had been putting the screws to the Indians with the help of his swell pal, Red Eye. Indian agency rations the government had sent west to be distributed free had been *sold*, not *given*, with the post commander discouraging other traders from undercutting Agent Colley's ever-so-fair prices.

Once you studied on it, it was small wonder Anthony had

gone back on Major Wynkoop's promise to issue army rations
if all else failed! Both the Bents and old Gray Blanket had been
potential rivals, who just might be able to scrape up more basic
staples for the Indians if they had to and the price was right.
Jim said, "Just imagine what Colley was demanding for government grub he didn't have to pay for, if he was afraid Smith
and the Bents could buy it wholesale, freight it all the way to
Fort Lyon, and *still* undersell him!"

I said I could surely see how swell things would have worked
out for the crooked Indian agent and his military business
partner if only the Colorado Volunteers had slaughtered *everyone* at Sand Creek. Since they hadn't, it seemed to me Anthony, Colley and company were in a whole heap of trouble.

Jim grimaced and said, "Mebbe. It's the word of an old
nigger repeating the word of a half-breed boy on the run with
his pretty little Magpie, and both the B.I.A. and U.S. Army
are inclined to take care of their own."

Getting the rest of the world to believe Colonel Chivington
and his boys had been used as bloody pawns at Sand Creek
wasn't the problem. Getting Colonel Chivington to believe it
was the problem. When we finally caught up with him in Denver
he simply refused to allow he could have been diddled, or that
his splendid victory could have been even a teeny-weeny mistake. He said he wasn't in the custom of *making* mistakes. I
suspect he believed this. I told him, "Colonel, if every officer
who's ever made a mistake had to line up for a whipping, Robert
E. Lee and U.S. Grant would be standing near the head of the
line! I was there with you. I know you thought you was doing
the right thing. I thought we was, too, albeit, no offense, I don't
talk to God personal as often as you."

Jim Beckwourth said, less gently, "I told you right off you
ought to let me ride in ahead and hear Black Kettle's side. But
what's done is done, John, and if you don't issue a statement
accusing Anthony and Colley, fast, you're fixing to wind up
with egg on your face, sure as hell. Bill Bent's as much a
reserve officer as you are, and he's already accusing you in
print of behaving like a total asshole down yonder!"

Chivington grimaced and said, "William Bent has a son running wild with Cheyenne crooked-lancers, even as we speak. Of *course* he'd like to make me look bad. I damned near finished off his precious Charlie, and we may still have to shoot his sweet little George! Whose word would you have me take, damn it, that of a half-breed actually riding with known hostiles or that of a fine fellow officer!"

Jim swore and insisted, "Damn it, John, them Indians were never hostile till just now, and Red Eye Anthony wouldn't make a pimple on a real officer's ass! He's a cowardly sneak who slickered you into killing his Indians for him, even when they didn't need killing!"

I suggested, "Can't you at least pull in your horns and calm down a mite, Colonel? You know my Martha admires you, but she says she and the other ladies find it sort of odd to hear a man of the cloth preaching death and destruction to the red race entire!"

Chivington drew himself up to reply, "Instruct the ladies to pay more attention to their Scriptures, then. An eye for an eye and a tooth for a tooth! Now hear the Word of the Lord! I never said anything about killing *every* Indian, by the way. I only want to wipe out all the Horse Indians, from the Comanche along the Mexican line to the Blackfoot up Canada way."

I told him that was mighty big of him and went on home to warm up the best way I knew how. Martha was glad as usual to help. But she said it was my own fault I'd near froze to death trying to help the mule-headed old cuss. Later, serving me scrambled eggs in bed, she said it would all blow over by New Year's, in any case.

She might have been right, if the Indians hadn't stayed so pissed. We later learned Black Kettle had lost so much *matou* that he'd slunk off with his wounded wife and a handful of other relations, leaving Leg In Water the paramount chief in our parts. So that was the end of Black Kettle as far as us Colorado Volunteers ever cared. But in case anyone's wondering, and because the two fights get mixed up when folk are weeping over Lo, the Poor Indian, that *was* Black Kettle, later, at the Battle of Washita in '67 when Custer and the 7th Cav found him holding white captives again. One of the hostages was drove permanently insane by all the gang raping and Custer finished Black Kettle off total, whether rightly or wrongly.

But getting back to the times of which I speak, we'd just gotten through Christmas, with business at my saddle shop pretty good, when Leg In Water led the South Cheyenne in an all-out winter campaign us old-timers still hate to recall.

They tore up telegraph lines and shot up wagon trains all across the frozen High Plains. A thousand Indians, or at least a whole lot of 'em, hit Julesburg, up where the South Platte crosses into Nebraska, with devastation in mind. So off went the Colorado Volunteers again. Only, when we got there, the Indians were gone, and so was Julesburg. Some of *them* women and children were cut up mighty ugly, too.

Then the Indians hit down along the Arkansas and now Red Eye *did* have his hands full. He sat on 'em, inside his fine fort, as Mr. Lo lifted hair and horses far and wide. By late winter we were suffering food shortages as well as general panic. Nobody will ever know how many lonely nesters went under, unrecorded, out on the lone prairie. Every time an Indian was taken alive, he bragged on all the hair he'd lifted in revenge for Sand Creek. So, slowly at first, like the first storm clouds on the horizon, some began to question just what might have *happened* down along Sand Creek, and why.

Witnesses like Gray Blanket and the Bents were only too glad to tell 'em and, in fairness to poor old Eagle Chief and at least half the boys, the opposition papers began to lay it on as thick the other way. I don't think there could have been two hundred killed, on both sides, during what was now "The Massacre of Sand Creek" and some of the things us drunken brutes were accused of doing were sort of tough to picture.

As it got less heroic to brag about having butchered babies, lots of old boys commenced to change their stories. When the army asked Red Eye what in thunder might have really happened, he implied the Colorado Volunteers had just surrounded his fort and taken over from him. Those in charge chose to buy his excuse. Some dubious reporters wondered when militiamen had commenced to order regulars around. It was let slip that *all* the officers and men connected in any way with the sad affair had been—what else—Colorado Volunteers, and, since the Firsters had their own honor to consider, they managed to convince a heap of reporters all the sons of bitches who'd murdered them women and children had been new recruits from the Bloody Third.

Through all of this, despite the advice of friends of foes, John Chivington refused to backtrack one inch, or even, for crissake, shut up. It was as if Robert E. Lee had insisted that dumb charge he'd ordered Pickett to try at Gettysburg had been a grand notion. Lee had long since allowed he'd made a mistake, and he was still running the Army of Virginia. Had he kept insisting Pickett's Charge had been a good move, everyone would have still been picking at it, like a scab. I'd told lots of folk in Denver that, yep, I'd been in the Sand Creek fight and, yep, it had been a real mess and, so far, it hadn't cost me any customers. But every time someone like John Smith or Bob Bent came up with another grim detail, the colonel would fire off a self-serving letter to the editor so dumb that you wanted to blush for him.

In sum, he kept it alive by refusing to let it die, and so, by that spring, a posse of fool congressmen came out to hold a hearing and get to the bottom of Sand Creek.

They never did. You've read how John Chivington was drummed out of the military in disgrace, stripped of his ministry by the Methodist Church, and so forth. But be it recorded that after hearing all the evidence, the congressional committee decided all concerned, save mayhaps the Indians, had acted in good faith. Tall Chief Wynkoop replaced Cooley and served with distinction as top agent to the South Cheyenne and Arapaho, once he got 'em calmed down again.

I don't recall what ever happened to Red Eye. The army has a way of sort of losing useless officers without it getting into the papers. Colonel Chivington simply resigned his commission. Some say Governor Evans asked him to. Others say he resigned in a snit after firing off another letter to the editor. He'd become so engrossed in defending his honor that even

Indian-haters took to crossing the street when they saw him coming.

When the Methodists dedicated their fine new seminary, which grew in time into the University of Denver, they didn't invite John Chivington to speak at the ceremony. I reckon they found it depressing to have a minister straying from the text of his sermon to warn about nits growing up to be lice. Martha, who took more interest in such matters, being a lady, said most Protestant congregations have more to say about their ministers than, say, Papists, and so poor old Eagle Chief wasn't so much defrocked as disinvited to say anything much until such time as he wanted to get back to religion.

I was there, with a handful of the old battalion, the day John Chivington boarded the coach out front of the Tremont House to go back to Ohio and sort of drop out of history. I don't think he noticed us as he boarded the coach, head proud but face pale. Jim Beckwourth still saluted him, so I figured I would, too. A pesky reporter, seeing the "Butcher of Sand Creek" off, noticed our almost meaningless gesture and recorded it as a freak of nature. It was printed in a paper we didn't subscribe to, but naturally a neighbor lady who did made sure my Martha saw what that fool darky and me had done.

Martha didn't mention it till she was serving me some of her swell peach cobbler that night. When she did, she asked about it casual, as if I'd made a harmless mistake with a banana peel, and she only wanted to know if I was all right.

I said, "To tell the truth I don't know why we saluted old John. He ain't an officer no more. But it seemed the right thing to do at the time. For in his day, John Chivington was one hell of a soldier."

She poured me some more coffee as she softly replied, "If you say so, dear. To hear some, he sounds more like a homicidal maniac."

To which I could only reply, "That's what I just said."

# About the Author

Lou Cameron created the "bible" for the popular *Longarm* western series. In 1976 he won the Spur Award for *The Spirit Horses*. Cameron is also a writer of crime novels.

His latest westerns for Fawcett include *The Buntline Special*, *Crooked Lance*, and *Yellow Iron*.